My throat's hoarse and stinging as I keep sc_____ ___ ___ _____ and tear away at the thick foliage. The trees and plants dance about and their colours shift from shades of red to blue and to green. And there are things in the air. Giant butterfly like creatures, I think, and other smaller ones too, swooping and buzzing about. I gouge my hand on a thorn again, don't feel much but see tiny maggots crawling and wriggling inside me. Don't know if they're real or not, don't know if any of this is? I slump down in a heap on the jungle floor, sobbing out her name.

"Rome... Rome... I'll find you little darling... Don't worry... Daddy will find you."

I'm crunched up in the foetal position with my eyes tightly shut, but don't see blackness. Bright colours and faces dance about like an awake, vivid dream. It's the flowers. These giant-like orchids that grow in and all around the jungle. Their sickly-sweet pollen is up my nose, in my eyes and down my damn throat. They squirt it out, day and night and I've figured it's a potent hallucinogen. I know that much… I think.

It doesn't make sense, none of it, and I can't piece it together. Last thing I remember is being with Rome, up above the planet, laughing and excited. Not only had we found a planet but we were the first ever, to find an intelligent one. Me, a half bit penny nobody from no-where. Remember looking down for the first time at these structures, giant like domes built with wood and knotted with rope, dotted about the landscape. And that was the last thing I remember. Don't know how long I've been here, don't know what's happened to my suit and I don't know when or how I lost Rome. They must have her, that's the only logical answer, but why and how did they take her and why would I take my damn suit off?

My suit, the gear that made me able to hop through space, which gave me oxygen and food and water, which was our communication to the other hoppers. It would have read the air was polluted and not safe to breathe in, so why would I discard it? Unless they took it like they took Rome, but how could they? They *are* intelligent but not *that* intelligent. If they had tried, we'd have just hopped off somewhere else, somewhere safe. Rome was above the planet with me? She was, she was!

Start climbing up the tallest looking tree I can see so I can take a good look about. Trying my best to avoid the huge thorns, dripping with that sick poison, slowly, but surely, I get right up in the canopy. Can't see much as the hallucinogen envelops the whole jungle in a purple-grey mist, but I can just see, further away, peaking out of the mist, a rocky hill with a peak. I'd be able to see all around from up there and maybe the pollen won't be as strong. I start descending back down the tree, but I lose my footing and slip. Bang my head on a branch and bump into others as I fall. I eventually crash onto the bottom of the jungle floor in a crumpled heap.

Had a peaceful childhood, and a protected one too, from "the sins of the big city" as Dad would always say. I was brought up in a neo-luddite community on an expanse of farmland where together, the community grew crops of rice, wheat, barley, and corn. Everyone would help, and everything was shared. Mum and Dad had their own personal bit of land too where they grew berries, apples, pears, and plums which they'd make into jams and chutneys. We'd always have vegetables as well, fresh from the ground and straight onto our plates. Had our own cow for fresh milk too, to churn homemade butter to spread on home baked bread and the larder was always stocked with mature cheeses, meats and preserves. Had a lot of chickens too so we always had fresh eggs and we had a pond with ducks and geese. Everything was natural, simple, and pure "as God had intended." I was taught.

In the wild forests I'd play hide and seek and up on the hills I'd fly kites. We had basic technology and no electricity. A horse and cart for transport, no television, no virtual reality and not even a phone. Life was good, peaceful, and protected as I said. Lazy days in the meadows filled with a lot of innocent fun, but from a young age, I always remembered having a hole in me that life just couldn't fill…that was until I met Cind.

I was by myself, on the outskirts of the woods exploring when I heard someone singing. I followed the voice, trying to be quiet, tiptoeing on the soft, green moss until I came into a glade surrounded by twisted trees. There I saw her, in a shaft of light with her back turned towards me but I couldn't believe what I saw with her. Around her, three tiny beings with transparent wings buzzed in the air above her head. It was true. I saw them with my very own eyes. Fairies!

I stepped forward, awestruck, needing to see them a little closer but as I trod, I snapped a twig. The fairies instantly vanished, and Cind turned sharply to face me. She had a pale freckled face with loops of blonde hair that fell down to her shoulders. I'd never seen anything prettier.

"Were you spying on me?" She asked.

"I'm sorry… I heard you singing… and followed you… I didn't mean to…spy…"

"Oh, it's OK. I was just playing with my friends."

"Where have they gone? I didn't frighten them, did I?"

"No, they're just back in the ball, waiting until I ask them to come back out again."

"They live in a ball?" I said. "Do *all* fairies live in *balls*?" She looked puzzled, like she was trying to figure something out.

"Are you from the village?"

"Yes."

"The village where people don't even have phones?"

"Yes."

"So, you don't have super-toys there?"

"What's a… *super-toy*?" She let out a sweet chuckle.

"Never mind. You can play with me if you like." She said tapping on the ball. They came back out and flew around again. They had tiny colourful clothes, tiny translucent wings, and tiny features. They darted about me and whispered questions in their tiny high-pitched voices.

"Who are you then?"

"You seem kind."

"Do you like stories about unicorns and dinosaurs?"

I was utterly mesmerised, the legends were all true and if they were, what else was? Magic? Dragons? Trolls? Or ghosts? It opened a new world to me where anything was possible and everything was magical. I stayed with Cind and the fairies that day, talking and playing until the sun dipped down. I fell in love with toys and technology then, and although I didn't quite know it yet… with a girl too.

My heads thumping as I come to from the fall. The jungle's swirling around and around and I'm cut and bruised. I don't feel much, but I don't think I've broken anything. I groan and get onto wobbly feet. Gotta get away from the pollen. Gotta to get to that peak. I hobble towards its direction, woozy, and as I do, my feet crunch on dried bracken and strange insect-like creatures the size of rats crawl out and stare at me. Can't be sure, but I think they're real. My belly's rumbling and I'm tempted to eat one, but my throat is bone dry and all I can taste on my stinging, cracked lips is the damn pollen. But food and water can wait. Gotta to find my suit. Gotta find Rome.

It takes a while but hacking and crashing through the thick foliage, I eventually get to the hill's rocky bottom. I scramble up the side and slip back and forth on the shale but after a few hours I manage to get to the top. Here, above the mist, I breathe in the air thankfully. The pollen still taints it, but it's much cleaner. Looking down I can see the top of a dome not too far away. About a quarter of a mile. That's where they are and I'm damn sure that's where my daughter is too.

"ROME! ROME! ARE YOU THERE LITTLE DARLING? ARE YOU THERE?" I shout out. But I know I'm kidding myself. Even if she were there, she wouldn't be able to hear me.

I come across a small cave opening and crawl inside. I rub my hands on its cool, moist, rocky walls and I lick at it. Feels like water but I could be drinking acid for all I know. The liquids dripping into a pool. I lie down and drink from it. It is water! I'm sure, and I gulp at it thankfully.

I wake up. Don't know how long I've been out for and I go for the water again. I'm not hallucinating now but I'm not feeling 100%. I start to look about the cave. Someone's been here before, *and* recently. In a corner there's empty food containers, loads of them scattered about the place. I go over and lick at them, but they're bare. Then I notice on the walls, paintings. Confusing, most of them, but one picture is of my damn suit. Definitely. The shape of it and the yellow and black colours makes it certain. Something's familiar. Could *I* have painted this? And above the pictures, there's these words painted in capitals- "IF I LEFT THE FOG" What does it all mean? Whose been here? The inhabitants, even if they don't have Rome, at least will know something. I have to go down and try and communicate with them, I have to go down to their dome.

    I skid on the shale again and once down, I see broken branches and trampled on ground. A path. A path that someone's made. Everything's not swirling around anymore but as I breathe, I can feel the damn pollen going deep into my lungs and deep into my veins again. Out of the blue, in an opening, an animal of some sort comes slowly plodding towards me. It has six legs and huge black eyes and there's good meat on it. I've *got* to eat, but should I? I have to! I run at it and grab a hold of it and wrestle it down to the ground, but it starts howling.

    "I'm sorry, I'm so sorry." I say with tears welling up. But it's either me or it. I pick up a stone. I need to do it, but it's looking back into my eyes, frightened, howling, and trembling, trying to get away from me. I can't. I just can't, but I must. I look up to the trees, crying, and see something up there. I shiver and let the stone fall from my hand. It's one of *them*. It's naked and all yellow except around its throat which is a lime green. It has two arms and two legs with long, skinny, fingers and long toed feet. It has a large, round head. But it's eyes. Big black ones, the size of grapefruits, with bright yellow irises look really panicked. Yellow, darting about in the black. From left to right and back again. I'm scared and I let the creature go from my grasp and it quickly runs towards the inhabitant which comes down from its tree. The creature leaps into its arms and they both embrace and the creature licks at the inhabitant's huge eyeballs with a long, purple, tongue. I think it's its pet or something, and it doesn't look happy.

    "I'm sorry. I'm just so God damn hungry" I say and point with my finger to my mouth. And at its neck, its throat box begins expanding and reverberating and it chirps and tweets at me, but menacingly. And then it points with its long-fingered hand at me and this deep red starts to engulf its black eyes, like blood clouding ink. And now I'm back in the cave. What's going on? I stumble around the cave, giddy and disorientated, whilst my belly's gurgling, eating away at itself. All the empty food containers are gone but in their place are two large orange pods. Someone else definitely *has* been here. But somehow time must be twisted, or something. I smell the pods. There's no scent to them, but when I break one open, there's bright, blue, flesh inside. I put my hand in, it's freezing cold and I scoop out some of the flesh and lick at it. It *is* food. Ice cold and bitter-sweet, like a lemon sorbet and I sit down, crying, but grateful, and eat away.

Cind and I became real close, real quick, but my parents didn't like the fact I had befriended someone who lived "sinfully". They tried to dissuade me, but I began to doubt their ways and their ideologies. What was wrong with electricity, virtual reality or synthed food? The one thing my parents would not take away from me was my freedom, and that meant freedom to wander through the forest, freedom to ramble up the hill and freedom to cross the stone, cobbled, bridge to Cind's home, and her home was real different to mine. We walked on ceilings with magnetic boots and flew around the meadow in jet-pack suits. We talked to depressed dogs and shared their troubles and saw through walls with x-ray goggles. We munched on chocolate popcorn synthed from the box and used detectors to find fossils hidden in rocks and we looked through telescopes at the infinite stars and took virtual trips on the plains of Mars.

That was something that intrigued and fascinated me. Something that went on and on, forever and ever and more. Mystical, fantastical, and practically virginal. Above me, and all around me, mesmerising me, and hypnotising me, the still black enticed and lured me like a maggot to a trout. That was where I was destined to go. That was where I belonged. To venture deep into, to search and find new worlds and discover new life. Although space exploration was the top sought after career and the hardest to join, that maggot wriggled wildly for me to take a bite. I knew I would have it, but although I didn't know it yet, something was about to get into young Arow's way.

One thing that even Cind's parents wouldn't let her use let alone me, was virtual reality. There had been incidents where VR simulations had caused serious mental illnesses, but a child's mind never thinks these things may happen to them, so when Cind's parents were away, we hooked into a 21-year-old certificate zombie shoot-em-up.

We went into a bare room, and as soon as Cind voiced a command, the whole room vanished and a concrete city strewn with upturned cars and smouldering buildings took its place. In my hands I marvelled as a gun materialised. It was solid, and even cool to the touch but as I saw them staggering towards me with blood-stained hands out to grab and drooling mouths out to bite, these feelings of awe quickly turned to terror. I fired my gun and missed a couple of times but on the third I got one in its belly. It jolted, and blood spattered into the air, but it didn't go down. It snarled at me and quickened its pace. I was scared, shit scared and I tried to shoot it as others came closer.

"CIND, I'M NOT SURE ABOUT THIS." I shouted above the noise, but she was too busy shooting the zombies coming for her. I turned back to shoot again but there was just too many and one of them dragged me to the ground. I needed to shoot it, but I couldn't. I was too damn scared.

"CIND! CIND! HELP ME! HELP ME!" I screamed as its teeth bit into my flesh.

"SWITCH IT OFF! SWITCH IT OFF!" I pleaded, rolling about on the concrete trying to throw it off. More hands grabbed at me. More teeth bit into me. Something was wrong, real wrong. I could feel pain. Real pain.

"THIS IS REAL! THIS IS REAL!" I screamed as blood spilled

from my wounds and pain stung all over my body, but then Cind shouted a command, and as quickly as it had all started, it all suddenly stopped and I was back in the bare room, on the bare floor. And then I heard Cind. She was laughing. How could she do that? How could she trick me and find it funny? This was all evil and so was she. I got up and ran out of the house wailing all the way across the meadow until I got to my house and sobbed the whole story to my parents. They had been right all along, and I knew now why they lived their way and I wanted nothing more to do with Cind and nothing more to do with her evil. And that was that, for the first time in my life my freedom was taken away from me and I was grounded for months and forbidden from ever seeing her again.

The days passed by, but slowly, and as I lay in my bed trying to read books and playing with my toys, I couldn't stop thinking about Cind and her game. Even though it had seemed real, it hadn't been. And even though I had felt pain, I was unharmed. I wasn't frightened now, and like Buddha enclosed in his palace protected from the real world, I craved for the forbidden even more.

So I practiced running around the forest with a potato gun firing at trees and flowers and my aim became as sharp as a sniper's and when I saw Cind, and she said she was really sorry, I said we could only stay friends if she'd let me have another go at the game. She said it was a really bad idea and she'd sworn to her parents to never play on it again, but after a few weeks of blackmailing, she eventually gave in.

This time, when it began, I didn't give them a chance. Shooting like a maniac I got them in the head with one shot and I revelled in it with not one ounce of fear. I must have killed a hundred or so when I became aware of her screaming, screaming of the like that I'd never heard before. As I turned to face her, I saw they were all on of her, feeding on her cheeks and gnawing on her arms.

"STOP THE GAME CIND. STOP THE GAME!" I shouted still firing.

"CIND. CIND. I DON'T KNOW THE COMMAND!" I shouted

out. I desperately tried to kill them, but there were just too many and as more came, swarming on her, she vacantly stared into my eyes.

"YOU LOSE. GAME OVER." The VR said emotionless and the game stopped and we were both back in the bare room. I ran over to her "Cind. Cind. Are you OK?" I sobbed cradling her in my arms. She was speechless, shaking.

"I'm sorry. It's my fault." I sobbed. "We shouldn't have gone on…we shouldn't have gone on!"

The sun has dipped and the moon has drawn over. I'm in my cave and my head's a lot clearer now. The water and fruit have done me good. So too has been being away from that damn pollen. But I can hear them. They're chirping and tweeting and clicking in the night. They're singing, but even though it sounds enchanting and mysterious, it makes me feel so damn angry.

"They have her…I know they do!" And I'm engulfed with rage. I've got to go down and see them. I run down the hill, shouting at them as I find the path in the dark. Rage is burning deep from within me, but no, I readjust my thinking, I *have* to stay calm. I *have* to stay quiet. I come closer to the dome and slow down and I creep, cautiously, and hide behind a white rock and watch.

Their dome is big. The roof must be over 30 feet high and God knows its diameter, maybe 800 or so. And I make out, under the middle of the dome, they've peeled back their roof somehow and a big, blue, moon beams down upon them. Like moon worshippers, they praise it and the stars with their singing. It's like a frog chorus.

I see loads of yellow ones, like the one I met with its pet. They're all over the place, hanging from the vines and rafters and laying lazily on the grassy ground. I notice a lot of them have different sized sacks, where a person genitalia are. They *are* a lot like us. But some of them seem to disappear into the very air itself whilst others appear from no-where. But there's other ones. White ones that are totally different to the yellows. Probably a different sex. They're massive, maybe 9 feet tall, with short, strong, stumpy legs. They lick at themselves with their huge tongues keeping their pure, white, skin clean, but at their throats, they're bright pink. That's how they're singing. Chirping and whistling through their vocal sacks. They breathe in and their air sacks inflate, and then they sing when their sacks vibrate.

I notice some of the white ones have huge, bulging, bellies. And they wear crowns on top of their heads made out of living vines and flowers, like the orchids, just smaller. Under the centre of the dome, under their skylight, slabs of rock lay, like standing stones, but they're upturned and point at different angles. Many of the white ones lie on top of the slabs, their arms and legs and fat bellies drooping over the stone's sides. But everything starts shifting around in colour and shape again, just whilst I'm getting to grips with them. That damn pollen. I feel giddy and sick and then I hear her. She's calling to me, "Arow…Arow…help me." Rage engulfs me and I run towards them under the dome shouting. "ROME! ROME! ARE YOU THERE?"

All their singing suddenly stops, and they all turn towards me and stare, hauntingly like I've interrupted something sacred.

"WHERE IS SHE?" I demand, but their eyes are so menacing and their irises shift about in different directions erratically.

"WHERE IS SHE?" I shout out, and then their black eyes are diluted by that blood red and I'm back in the cave. Is it the damn hallucinogen? No. I know now, I've figured them out. One minute I'm here and the next I'm not, and the yellow ones were disappearing and reappearing. Somehow, they can teleport.

Cind was eventually able to move and we left the VR room and stumbled to the forest and lay silent on the cool grass, staring at the clouds. Eventually, she spoke.

"I couldn't do anything. I couldn't even speak to turn it off. And now I'm scared. Scared of everything. I mean I've never really thought about dying, but now I can't *stop* thinking about it. If Hell and the Devil and demons are all true and if that's where I might go?

What if they *are* Arow?" She said "And what God would ever let that be? But above it all, I saw you more concerned about me than yourself, trying to save me. I'll always remember that Arow and you'll always be my best friend." She said and then gave me a kiss. We stayed up that night, out in the meadow staring at the stars and talking about the big whys and buts until our parents found us and took us home. Unfortunately, many people when they are young and naive can have their paths in their lives steered to a completely different direction. At the age of 12, both of us, for the good or the bad, were no longer kids.

We never did go back on that game, but whenever we got the chance, we'd plug into many other safe ones. Something about the VR enticed and excited me and real life was just too damn boring. Why would I want to play in the meadow or fish in the river when I could fly above cities and battle with super villains, dance on strange worlds with bizarre looking aliens, swim in warm lava pools, in the centre of the Earth, or watch extinct animals giving multiple births? But then my whole world collapsed. Cind's parents got new jobs and she moved away. I was devastated. Not only had I lost my best friend, but I'd lost a whole world of gadgets and gizmos too. I grew bitter, and discontent with stale home baking and boring wooden games. Time did pass, but very slowly, and I was alone and miserable.

I made a pal who lived in the city who liked to plug in to VR too so whenever I could, I would go over to his. I couldn't walk there though as it was too damn far, so I'd either blag a lift or lie to Mum and Dad for cash for a bus. They weren't daft though, and no matter how much I argued with them that the VR was harmless, they stuck firm to their beliefs. It went on like that, arguing, getting grounded, lying and even one time me and Dad ended up in a fist fight. As soon as my 16th birthday came, I packed a suitcase, hopped on a bus and was off. I got a little council studio with bed, shower, kitchen, box, and basic VR. I didn't have to work so I sunk deeply into my virtual world. At last. I had made it.

With the box I synthed whatever I wanted to eat and drink and through my VR I plugged into any reality I liked. I began using it daily but unknown to me, it had started to consume me. I shut myself off and for three years, I practically didn't see anybody. I said that I had moved and never answered the door and didn't even bathe or dress. I had lost all hope and my only real honest ambition was to go to space. I would plug into the planets and feel the winds and touch the rocks and ice on the barren, lifeless worlds and I would marvel at the black holes, new suns, dwarfs, moons and cosmic dust and watch the stars die and be born. But what really gave me a kick, were the two planets that they'd found which had life on them. I swam in the cold seas with the colossal single celled organisms on the first planet. They were just starting off, and I pondered the speed of evolution and what they would eventually become. And on the second planet, where life had already had millions of years to evolve, I watched, fascinated by the magnificent wind beasts, climbing up the steep rocks and using their facial wind sacks, to suck air in and out of their hollow limbs to firmly stick to the rocks and catch monkey-birds in mid-flight. And it had such diverse insect life too, tiny, but so colourful and busy, building grand yellow, orange, red, and black sandcastles on the beaches to trap and consume small crustaceans as the green, foamy waves lapped in and into their traps. But now reality and unreality had merged into one. I could not tell what was real from the unreal. I came to in a detox centre when coincidentally, they found and landed on a third planet with life. "Beso" they called it and its name rolled of my tongue. From sweat, soaked, sheets, cold and shivering, I watched the astronauts land, on the safety of a telly as they filmed the aliens.

   All of the different creatures there lived off the lava. The weaver creatures would spin sails to ride on the lava's heat to slowly float up high to unreachable cliffs and crevices to graze on the mosses and lichen. And the slow, sloth like creatures, would bend over the lava pools and inhale their fill of gases through their large, expandable mouths and then collapse and sleep for days. I had to have a piece of this, I just *had* to, so when I was fit enough, I went back to Mum and Dad's and did hard labour on the farm. I ate well, exercised, and began looking after myself and you know what? I actually started to appreciate their ways more. Fresh veg from the ground *did* taste better, especially when you took part in growing it. I built fences and barns, sheared the sheep, painted walls, dug the dirt, and looked after the bees, everything and anything to keep me occupied, and after a year, I moved back to the city and started college. With my new understanding of the perils of hedonism, whilst other students were partying, I stayed in reading books and watching telly. I was proud to become 3rd in my class and I got accepted in a small space academy. New advances were coming out daily. Teleportation came out. Real, fucking, teleportation! Within 2 years you could hop to any country through tele-booths and the space academies developed it for their ships too. Millions of miles of space, scanned, then bypassed by hopping through it. And it was contagious and spread and accelerated like wildfire. Hundreds more academies formed letting thousands more venture into space and I was going to have a piece of it. I was bright, happy, hopeful, and optimistic, not just about my life, but for the whole world... but things were going to take a darker turn.

I was pushing weights in Charlie's when I noticed a familiar, sweaty face jogging on a treadmill. I had to look twice. "Was it?" Half from my work out and half from the butterflies flapping around my belly, I stumbled over to her feeling drunk.

"Cind?"

She looked at me, then it registered with her and she punched the treadmill to a stop.   "AROW!"

I wake up in my cave and I rub at my sore eyes. Something is here. There's a yellow one, perched up on a rock, staring at me. I jolt, scared shitless. I think it's the same one that was with its pet.

"What do you want?" I say and it chirps and then points at the paintings. I wait. And we just stare at each other. I look deep into its large, black eyes. In their centre, there's swirls of yellow and orange. It reminds me of buttercups.

After some time I say, "That's what I'll call you. 'Buttercup'" and I point at myself and say my name. It chirps back at me, its lime green vocal sack inflating and deflating, purring like a kitten. And then he points in the corner next to me. He points at more pods and then he opens his enormous, toothless mouth and points inside it. I know what he's saying.

"Thankyou." I say and I'm more at ease. He wants to feed me and I don't think he means me any harm; I think he's here to help. I walk over and with a struggle, break a grey-blue one open. There's red flesh inside and I try and pull a bit off, but it's too damn tough. I use my teeth and gnaw at it and manage to get a mouthful. Its's delicious, meaty, and juicy, like a rare fillet steak. Whilst I eat, Buttercup stays perched on his rock and looks upwards towards the pink sky.

After I've only eaten a quarter, I'm full to the brim and I make a gesture to see if he wants some. He shakes his head; we *are* communicating and he *does* understand. He comes down off his perch and comes towards me. I'm not scared now; I know he wants to help. He picks up the other fruit and using his long fingers he twists off the top in a oner and hands it to me and makes a hand signal to his mouth to drink from it. Thirsty, I laugh, "Thank you." I say, and drink from the opening. It's delicious. Like really strong, blackcurrant juice, and ice cold too. After I take a couple of swigs, I hand it to him. And when I do, his sack reverberates really low, chuckling like a belly laugh and he takes it and takes a swig and we both just start laughing together. It's beautiful, I'm communicating to the first, ever found, intelligent life, for the very first time.

Buttercup waves one of his long fingers in the air and then points to the fruit. He's trying to tell me something. His black eyes then get engulfed in that blood red again, and from his left hand, the fruit vanishes, and after a few seconds, it reappears in his right. I was right…they *can* teleport, and they can teleport objects too. Then he chirps and tweets at me and points to the painting of my suit, and the other images and then to the words, "IF I LEFT THE FOG." He goes over to it and taps on the painted letters.

"What is it?" I ask, "What are you trying to tell me?" He keeps tapping at the strange phrase on the wall and then he points outward from the cave and downward, I'm sure, down to the dome.

"Rome?" I question, and he looks at me, like he understands, "Rome? Where?" and he walks out of the cave and I follow. Then he laughs that deep, reverberating laugh again and points up to the sky and I'm sure when he chirps, he's saying my daughter's name. Then he looks back at me, and his eyes turn that blood red, and he vanishes.

Cind was a party girl and had loads of friends. Ironically, she was working only blocks away from my place in a small caf. She said she had always wondered how I was doing and was waiting for the day we would "naturally" bump into each other. We went out that night and wined and dined and caught up over lost days, and then we went back to her place and made love. I knew we had always meant to be, but she really *was* a party girl. During the night, a man, stark naked jumped into bed with us. She called it "free love", with anybody and everybody. Confused and distraught, I left. She was always meant to be mine and mine alone, wasn't she? In the weeks that followed I met all her wacky friends, sniffing the latest off each other's backs and dancing and getting body morphs in the orgy clubs. Anything went, the madder and badder the better, and even though I loathed it, I was drunk in love with my 5 foot 5, curly blonde, blue-eyed goddess, no matter how weird and dangerous her ways were. So I tried to show her another life, to change her ways, but she wouldn't listen, so I told her parents about her problems to try and get it through to her but that just really pissed her off. So I stuck to my studies and read bigger books and pushed bigger weights and I excelled in programming. But seeing Cind and the way she was, stress took a hold and I started using a little VR as medication! I only used an hour a day at first but then one became two and two became eighteen and quickly I was back to being an unkempt, isolated, completely lost addict. When I came off it again, this time was worse. Through withdrawals, I had a major breakdown. "VR psychosis" they called it. I remembered little about the months of hospitalisation and medication it took to get me back on my feet. I vaguely remembered family and Cind coming to see me and when I was finally fit enough, I went back to the academy to start where I had left off. But when I got there, they said they had wanted to speak to me in person. They said with my condition "I wasn't going to be suitable" as "What would happen if you broke down in space?" I tried applying to other academies, but it was the same response, I was too high a risk and that was that. I'd lost my mind, my dream was in tatters, and the final nail in my coffin, Cind hammered in when she said, "seeing you like that made me evaluate *my* life" and she had got such a shock she had decided to change *her* ways. Now *she* was going to join the space race and she had already been accepted into an academy. I was bitter, damn bitter and started seeing less and less of her as she trained. I went back to the farm and tried to get my mind in order. I'd work through it. I'd study. I'd do anything. Somehow, someway, I'd make it into to the black.

When I did meet up with Cind, I felt as though I had become an unwanted hanger-on and as the years passed and she majored in space botany, my bitterness grew. It was when she told me that she was due to go on one of the hopper ships on a one-way mission on an uncharted path that I broke down crying in her arms. Even though we'd been through such bad times, I couldn't imagine never seeing her again. So I booked the most romantic hotel in Rome that I could afford and with flowers and sobbing over a 5-course meal, I pleaded with her not to go. She said I was getting pathetic, but drunk, and with her feeling sorry for me, we went to bed. When I woke, she was gone. Over a month went by without a word, but then out of the blue, she rang and said she was leaving in a week but wanted to stay at mine for one last night as she needed to talk and "clear something up."

Then a thought came. I'd read about this new technology where you could scan a person and make a virtual copy of them. Not just any old basic hologram that looked and talked and walked the part, this way you copied their DNA, their very own consciousness. It had already been banned in most countries but with my skills with programming I could synth the parts without anyone ever knowing. The thought of Cind's copy being just as pissed as the real Cind didn't deter me. I could turn her off or re-programme her to want to stay with me. It was wrong, on all levels, but she was going away and would probably be never coming back. The real Cind could never find out though, that was for certain. I was being desperate and irrational, but I just couldn't bear to live without her. If there was a chance, I *had* to try. I synthed the parts and put it all together, but just before she arrived, sanity flooded back. I *had* stooped low, but I wasn't going to stoop any lower. I threw the gear into the back of my cupboard and looked forward to our night. When she came over, she told me her news. That night, when she was drunk in Rome, for some reason her pills hadn't worked. She was pregnant and there was no two ways about it, she wasn't going to have it.

"Please Cind…please...I'm begging you...at least think it over."

"No Arow, I leave in a week. I'll stay, but just enjoy this night. Our last night."

I stayed up not being able to stop my head screaming. My dream of going to space was shattered, my lover didn't want to be with me and she was going to live my dream and I would never see her again. And my child, *my* unborn child was not going to be because Cind held all the cards because she was a she. No future. No love. No chance of a family. But then an insane but intriguing thought niggled into my mind. What if I didn't use the scanner to copy Cind? What if I used it to copy our unborn? I knew that it was wrong but I couldn't stop thinking about it, so as she lay there sleeping, I went to my cupboard, got the gear out, and quietly scanned her tummy.

I need to find out where Rome is and to do that, I need to go down to their dome. And I know that going down there in a rage just doesn't work so I've got to try and fight the pollen. I walk down the shale, slowly this time. It's light now and the sky is a bright pink and the clouds are like candy floss. I get to that rock again and this time settle myself down comfortably.

The yellows are milling about and swinging on the rafters and appearing and reappearing. They're like little, muscular, kids, but they're not just playing. I see a white one quite close to me and get a good look at her. She's laying there on a slab of rock covered in blue vines for bedding and she's donned in flowers. They're all over her and seem to have suction pads that feed of her wet, glistening body. She's slouched there, lazily, whilst a yellow one is peeling pods and feeding them to her. She's like a lazy queen and the yellow is caring for her every need like a butler. Her belly's really big and something is inside. I can make out movement and shifts in shades of colour, but the pollen is starting to kick in so I can't be sure. I've got to stay calm and overcome it. I've got to try. I take a deep breath and slowly trod towards her. They immediately all notice me and stare, so I freeze, and put my hands up peacefully.

"I don't mean you any harm." I whisper and take another step. They keep watching but don't teleport me as I take more steps and get closer to her. Her belly *is* translucent, and something *is* inside. Something alive, but not like them. Something different. It seems to have multiple limbs like some sort of large, weird, fat, millipede. It's unnerving.

Everything's swaying again and a yellow one startles me by suddenly jumping from a vine and landing right in front of me. It's Buttercup and he waves his hands at me and ushers me towards the white one. There, he breaks open a pod, scoops the flesh out, and gives it to her. She swallows it whole and licks her lips and then immediately chirps for more. Buttercup nods at me and picks one up and hands it to me. I've gotta play along with this. If I can just do that, then maybe I'll find Rome. I grip it, and after a few attempts, I manage to twist the top off. Then I do the same as Buttercup and start scooping the flesh out and hand feed it to the white who swallows and then chirps for more like a ravenous, eager, eaglet. There's a huge pile of the pods next to her, and she's hungry. But halfway through the second pod, I start hearing Rome, calling to me, but I get on with my job in hand. It isn't Rome, it's the damn pollen. But the white one I'm feeding starts to change in looks and demeanour too. She becomes this scary and repulsive monster with horns and tails forever demanding food. I hear Dad calling too whilst she wants more and more. These fruits she's eating, is just her starter. The main meal is me. But no. Fight it. It's just the damn pollen. As everything swirls and shakes about, I dump the half-eaten pod and run back to my cave. And I stay there, breathing in the cleaner air, petrified.

It was awkward, and I was damn nervous about Cind waking, but after a few minutes, the scanner finished copying. I read some of the data, it was a girl! I clicked the button and there she appeared. She must have only been a centimetre long but I enlarged her to get a better look. Her whole lower body was a tail. Legs or arms hadn't formed but she had eyes even though they we're only small, dark discs and she had a brain, and a beating heart. Had I acted irrationally or wrongly? No, of course I hadn't. This was life, and this was my right. Cind stirred in her sleep so I quickly switched my virtual unborn off and put her on a stick which I hid in my back pocket and nervously began to wipe any data from the scanner.

"What are you doing?" Cind said sleepily. She saw me with the scanner and stared at it for a few seconds until it registered with her.

"You bastard, you copied me, didn't you? You know that's been banned, don't you? You did you creep didn't you! Where is it?" She said grabbing the gear and frantically typing buttons to see what was stored.

"I was about to…sorry…I just couldn't live without you. But I didn't. Please believe me. I didn't copy you. Just stay with me... Please."

"That's it Arow. That's the final straw. DID, YOU, COPY, ME?"

"No, I swear I didn't, I swear." Her lips trembled with rage as she glared at me. Then she grabbed the scanning gear and smashed it against the wall.

"You creep, go and get a life." she said and quickly got dressed and was off in a maddened-bitter-whirl. When I calmed down and I knew she wasn't coming back, I turned her back on. And there she appeared, floating in the air. I moved my fingers through her intangible body and head, and sat there, hypnotised by her tiny beating heart. And that's when I thought of the perfect name for her.

"Rome? Rome? Can you hear me little one? Don't you worry now, everything's going to be fine, Daddy's going to look after you."

I wake up in my cave. I feel woozy, hot, damp, and hungry. There's another pod waiting for me but Buttercup is nowhere to be seen. I crack it open and eat whilst staring at the paintings and the ominous words, "IF I LEFT THE FOG". Did I write this? Or did someone else? The lettering looks familiar, somehow. Even if I did or did not write this, it has to mean something but I just can't remember. And the more I stare at the paintings, the more frustrated I get. As well as my suit, there seems to be figures. Yellow ones and white ones and a large black figure too. I can't stay here any longer. My minds gnawing away at itself. I've gotta go down and play their game.

I go down the hill and onto the path and walk to their dome. There's not so many of them there today. Fewer yellows and fewer fruit. The white one I was feeding is fast asleep on her rock. Most of the white ones are asleep, or at least dozing. Some of them raise their heads, but then lay them back down seeming uninterested and exhausted. They must be getting used to me.

I stroll about and check out the whites. I can practically see straight though their bellies and to the creatures that are inside. Some with wings, some with legs and arms and some with flippers and gills. The pollen starts to take its toll though. But I've gotta fight it.

I wander further to the centre, but a yellow appears out of nowhere and pushes me back. Does he not want me to see something? I go back to the white one who I was feeding and lay next to her. I'll concentrate, I'll meditate, even if it kills me, I'll beat this. Time goes by as I lay next to her and I touch her belly with the multi-limbed creature moving about inside of her. She raises her head and stares at me and then nods back off. I put my head on her belly. It's wet and warm and I can hear her heartbeat slowly thump, thumping. It's comforting and I stay there, relaxed, and calm until I hear a mighty cacophony. Loads of yellows have appeared and they're surrounding a giant pile of pods. They're harvesting them, but where from?

I see Buttercup with his pet around his neck. He seems happy to see me and chirps and tweets at me and jumps up and down pointing to the pile of pods proudly.

"God, I wish I could understand you." I laugh, but I'm happy at his happiness. They all start sharing out the pods, carrying them and dividing them into smaller piles next to the whites. A lot of them are taken towards the centre, I mean a lot, but when I try and see exactly where to, Buttercup ushers me back. What *are* they hiding? My suit? I've got to somehow get there and find out.

I start peeling the pods again and feed them to the white. But when I get to the second, I can feel the pollen kicking in. I leave and rush up the shale to my cave whilst I fight of the unreal sounds and images and fears.

"They're delusions. They're damn delusions." I say again and again to myself. I breathe in the cleaner air and drink from my pool of water whilst I hear Rome's voice crying out to me. I fight it. It's false, it has to be, and after an hour of going mad, she eventually quiets. I'm beating it, and I go back down to feed the whites again. My tolerance to the pollen is getting stronger.

I needed to find out everything about my virtual unborn, so I began searching. Even though the technology was only in its infant stages, there was a wealth of info and even a term had been coined, "Virtual Beings" or "VB's" they called them: Man creates VB of deceased wife. Lonely woman creates VB of herself. Man imprisoned for creating thousands of copies of himself to beat mortality. It went on and on and even though it was illegal, it wasn't stopping people doing it, and everyone was talking about it. Was it wrong? Had we gone too far or was this the next stage of man's evolution? Whatever individual's opinions were, people were scared. I searched on and on but I started to become fearful as I found no information of someone scanning a foetus like I had. Frantically I searched through page after page for at least a shred of information of someone doing what I had… but no-one had. The only exception were scientists who'd copied animal foetuses. As it began to dawn on me that I may have done the unthinkable it was as though Rome was somehow connected to my distress too. At first her colour changed a darker red and her tail began wiggling, but then her whole body became rigid and her tail began thrashing. "What is it? What have I done?" I said nervously. I brushed my fingers through her and sung her a nursey rhyme but this made her thrash even more. Then she turned an angry-purple and let out a tiny high-pitched moan. She was only a month old; how could she even move let alone moan? I knew then how little I knew about a real unborn let alone a virtual one. How long was I going to keep her like this? 8 months with no nourishment given from an umbilical cord, no comfort or safety from the warmth of a womb, no presence of a loving mother through sight, sound, touch, or emotion. This room was her womb. The power supply was her womb. I was her womb!

"NO! NO! NO!" I shouted out hitting at my bare walls as her moans became squeals. I couldn't listen to her, I needed time to think so I switched her off as my thoughts became darker and darker whirring around my head in an incessant, agonizing, non-winnable debate. Would she ever have a normal life? Would she always be in pain? Had I done what should never have been done? There was no right answer, I *had* gone against the laws of nature I knew pacing around my room. She couldn't exist like this, I knew that. I had to do something, but what? Then a simple revelation came to me. I couldn't keep her in an infant stage like this, in torment and agony, what I needed to do was comfort her with words and wisdom to see what *she* wanted, and I knew I couldn't wait years for her to develop "naturally". I needed to fast-forward her growth.

Scientists had done tests on virtual rat and monkey embryos where they'd fast-forwarded their biological clock to see how their minds and bodies were affected by diseases and social ecosystems over life spams. I knew she wasn't a rat, but I could copy basic codes and mix them with human data, couldn't I? I stayed up for days, adding and mixing, copying, and pasting, filling in gaps, but it was like an unsolvable puzzle. When should I let "nature" take its course and when should I not? What about her features? Her memory? Her emotions? Her socialisation? Could she get diseases? Has she real DNA? Should she have 100% memory? Was that right? How much anger, 10 % or none at all? What use has anger anyhow? Her senses, her damn senses, that was the key, no, her consciousness was or were they not both entwined? On and on I sweated with blurry codes of data in my vision, sometimes feeling like a worried father on a heroic mission and at other times like a maddened Victor Frankenstein. After 4 nights, exhausted beyond belief, I eventually had some sort of programme I could test on her.

"What would she become?" I thought. "Should I really do this?" There were no two ways about it, I had made her and I could not murder her so I punched the download button and switched her back on.

The days go by and melt into each other. I feed the white ones and when I breathe in too much pollen, I go back to my cave, recuperate, and then go back to the dome. It's taking longer and longer for the pollen to affect me and I can walk freely around them now, apart from the dome's centre. What are they hiding from me there?

One day, the yellows all surround a white one who is bulging at the seams. She has some sort of humongous tadpole like creature, swimming about inside of her and she looks like she's ready to pop. The brawny yellows get her onto her feet and support her and walk her like a disabled, elderly person towards the middle of the dome, but as I try to follow, Buttercup pushes me back. I try and see through the crowd and over the rocks and through the foliage and can just make out that the yellows making a ring, surrounding something, something big. And then all their eyes are flushed with that red, and they vanish.

Buttercup allows me to go to where they hopped from. There are hardly any yellows there now and I wonder where they have gone and what they are up to? Something important I feel. There's bright coloured foliage growing in the centre and many orchids. Buttercup grabs one and without breaking the stalk, pulls it down towards his mouth and drinks the pollen from it. When all is drank, he licks at it, cleaning up every last bit of it with his huge tongue. It's almost like it's a delicacy to him. Then he pulls another one down and offers it to me. I shake my head, but he doesn't seem to understand. The pollen, I'm sure, even though it is the cause of my misery, is vital in their world. Of what magnitude, I am yet to find out.

Rome appeared in the centre of my living room still a demented purple colour with her tail thrashing about wildly. I voiced the programme to begin and a virtual womb materialised and enveloped her. Sitting in my armchair, biting my nails, I watched her on a screen. Gleaming, virtual, amniotic fluid materialised, bathing her in colour, and a thin virtual umbilical cord materialised and connected to her belly. Virtual rich blood pumped in and out of her body, but her violent spasms seemed to only worsen. I began the fast-forwarding. A minute would be like a day to her, so if everything went to plan, she would be born in around 4 hours.

"Please, I know I have never prayed to you before, but if you are there, just let this work."

Everything began quickening. Her heart began beating in the blink of an eye and bright fluid shot in and out of her, dazzling, then fading, like thousands of falling shooting stars. Her tail wiggled violently back and forth and split off into two stumps. Shaking legs and juddering arms formed, but it was so damn hard to make out. Feet and hands appeared as the womb gurgled. Time passed, but it was all in a blur. Her head grew bigger and bigger but would shake for a few seconds, then stop and then shake again. I couldn't watch her any longer so I went and lay in my bed sweating and praying. The clock eventually reached 3 hours and 22. She'd be around the 8 months mark now but what would happen if she was naturally meant to be premature, or even late? I ran back and watched her. In a fraction of a second, again and again, her mouth opened and then snapped shut whilst her feet kicked, and her hands clawed at the womb's sides. I couldn't take it anymore. I knew she was in torment so I voiced the programme to stop and shaking with apprehension, I looked at the screen. She looked like any other new-born, but she was still red and rigid. I was numb with fear as I voiced the womb to disappear and a virtual cot, with a virtual cotton blanket materialised. Screaming, she slowly sank down into the cot.

"What have I done?" I said and knew that I would have to switch her off for good. I stumbled to my feet, giddy and sick, ready to end it when I realised… she wasn't screaming. There she was, calm and staring up at me. I broke down weeping as I looked at her looking back at me. She had little wisps of hair and tiny fingers and tiny toes. Shaking, laughing hysterically I stroked her soft, pink skin and she stirred to my touch. It *was* working. In the VR I could feel her and she could feel me. I gently picked her up and put my pinkie in her mouth and she made clucking noises as she sucked. A feeling that everything was going to be alright flooded over me and I sat down, mesmerised. Then my intercom buzzed. My short joy instantly changed back to fear. I tried to ignore whoever it was but they weren't giving up so I switched Rome and the VR off, and nervously answered the intercom. It was Cind!

"Hey you." I said dozily pretending to have just woken. She looked upset.

"Can you let me in, I need to talk."

"It's actually not the be..."

"I, *need*, to, talk!"

"OK, OK." And I hesitantly buzzed her in.

As soon as she entered, she broke down.

"What is it, what's happened?"

"I had the abortion." She sobbed. "It was a girl Arow. I murdered our little girl."

I didn't know what to say. I just cuddled her as she cried.

"You were right Arow. I should have kept her." She said, "And there was a complication too."

"What? What complication? Are you hurt?"

"No, not in a way. I'm still fit enough to leave. You'll be there, won't you? At my take-off?"

"Yes. Of course I will. But what's happened? "

She looked deep into my eyes and then shook her head, "I'm sorry I can't do this," she said. "I shouldn't have come."

"Wait Cind. Stay for a while. Please."

"I can't Arow, I just needed to see you before I go." And as quickly as she had arrived, she left.

I thought about the abortion and about Rome. Should I tell Cind about her? It could be medicine for her pain. No, it was too risky, she could easily be appalled, and she was leaving on a one-way ticket into the depths of the unknown anyway. I couldn't risk tainting her dream and I couldn't risk Rome's safety. I turned her back on and held her in my arms. She was so beautiful, perfect, and innocent, but I knew I couldn't keep her like this. At some point, I would have to run the second stage of my programme.

I'm there when they hop back. Buttercup had previously ushered me away from the dome's centre, somehow knowing their arrival.

Two of the yellows are at either side of the huge white one, holding her long arms, supporting her as she hobbles back to her slab of rock. Exhausted, she collapses onto it and immediately falls asleep. She's taken an absolute pounding. And when I go to her and see her belly, it's all flabby and saggy where the tadpole creature was.

The yellows have hopped somewhere with the white and her creature. She was nurturing it, surely. And the creature has gone. Maybe the more yellows there are, making that ring, gives them more energy to hop somewhere far off. But why do they grow these creatures in the first place and where do they go?

I go back to feeding the whites, bored and anxious, and full of unanswered questions. I've got to be patient and somehow find out what they're hiding or protecting underneath the dome's centre. I have to find my suit. I have to find Rome.

One bright, fresh day, I see something that helps me get the bigger picture. The sacks, that many of the yellow ones have growing between their legs, gets that big and ripe on one of them that he pulls it off. I wince, empathising with him, but he isn't in any pain. And then he picks it up, goes over to a white, and slips it into her. Into her pouch, brimming with that liquid. The white is kind of like a marsupial. The yellow ones are creators and the white ones are growers. Together they create new life, and nurture it. That's what they're doing, but where the Hell are they taking them to? I go back to my cave to think.

"IF I LEFT THE FOG." I can't stop staring at the phrase. It's telling me to leave. Surely. Away from the fog and maybe to the other inhabitants underneath a different dome? They may have my suit or at least know something about it. I have to find out. I have to try and go. It will take a while, maybe quite a long while as the other domes are miles away, and I will have no safety from the clean air in my cave. I might be consumed by the pollen, I may go permanently insane...but I have to try.

Cind's ship took up the space of three football fields. Golden, with a jet-black frame, it glinted in the bright sun as the astronauts paraded towards it. Myself, 700 family members and friends, all sat in an area wishing our last, silent farewells. On a screen we could see them as they trod on their home world's soil for possibly their last time. I just saw Cind when I got a hard slap on my back.

"Alright Arow, haven't seen you in a while, how's your old noggin doin'?"

"OK." I said. This guy I remembered was a real pain and I couldn't even remember his name.

"You must be real down she's going? Heard you left on pretty bad terms?"

"No offence, but it's really none of your business." I said and tried to ignore him as the astronauts entered their ship.

"Big shame what happened to her wasn't it? That nurse was downright *evil*. Sure the journey will do her good though."

Suddenly interested, I said "What nurse?"

"What, you didn't know? Thought she would have told *you*. Where have you been for the past week anyhow? It's been all over the news.... Dreadful business it was. She was pregnant and didn't want the kid but the nurse that was doing the abortion...what was her name again...an Ismie...an Ismie Right I think, yes…you really don't know, I thought both of you were real tight?" I let him go on as the ship's doors shut.

"She burnt her. Apparently hundreds of others were done before she was found out. "

"Burnt her?"

"Yeah, her ovaries man. Her fucking ovaries. A nurse working in an abortion clinic! The irony man. Thought it was all the Devil's work."

As he wittered on my mind went blank and I didn't even notice the countdown beginning. When it got to one and the ship was engulfed in white, crackling, light and vanished, all I could feel was a deep sadness. That was what the "complication" had been, Cind was off into the depths of space and would never be able to have children.

    I don't know how long it will take me to get to another dome. I don't know where or how far one is, but if I try and walk in a straight line, and climb up the trees to scout about, I'm hoping I'll find one. And if I get close to one, the other inhabitants may find *me*.
    I eat as much as I can of a pod and drink my fill of water and descend down the hill. Then I go in the opposite direction of the path. Straight away it is daunting. The vegetation is thick and tough and branches and thorns stick out from everywhere. I'm quickly cut and sore, but I hack away at it and go on. God could I do with a machete. After what seems like a couple of hours, I carefully climb a tree. I get high up enough, but all I can see is the jungle and my hill which is still close by. This is madness, and everything already is starting to swirl.
    I get back down safely and trek on but I hear whispers, faint at first, of home and of close ones sweetly calling to me and then the whispers turn to voices. Of Rome and then of Cind and then of my parents. I fight them. I know it's the pollen, but I'm not sure. It sounds and seems so real. Out of the jungle itself she appears. Rome. It *is* her. Her beautiful face and sweet, sweet voice, saying how happy she is that I've found her, and now at last, everything will be fine. And I see Cind too. She's comes from her planet. To be with me and to be with Rome, and she's saying it's taken her such a long time, but she's so glad she's finally here. I'm overcome, ecstatic and crumple into a heap on the floor, sobbing. This *is* real! And my parents come out of the jungle too. Overjoyed to see me again and they cuddle me and comfort me.
    "You'll make it Arow…just stay here, with us." My Dad says.
    "NO, NO, NO." I cry, this can't be real, how could it be, *you* are here. I've got to define between what is false and what is not, but it's too damn tricky. For hours I go hacking and thrashing through the wild trying my best to ignore them. I'm tired, and hot and cut and

whipped by the thorns and branches. I can't do this. I just can't. But could they all really be here with me right now?

"NO. YES. NO. YES." I shout to myself as I stumble on. No, this is *not* real, and I have to find my real Rome.

It gets dark and I can't see a thing in front of me, but I start to hear something. I trample further, yes, I hear them. The other inhabitants. It is them, their chirps and tweets are irrefutable. I hack on, towards their singing. Their worshipping of their moon and their stars. I've found them, and I'm close. Real close. But I've already found Rome, and she is safe and happy and at peace. I must stay with her and protect her. No. Fight it Arow. Fight it.

I crash on, hacking at the foliage harder, quicker, frantic to see them. And over a rock, and underneath the moonlight I find their dome. I slow down, they've never seen me before so I need to be calm. They look the same as the others. The whites, with their pink throats lazing about and the yellows, with their green throats, inflating and deflating. But it's too familiar. The dome looks exactly the same. I tread towards them, and a yellow sees me and advances towards me. He has his pet. The same pet. It's Buttercup, and I have gone in a complete circle. He chirps at me, but I vomit and stumble back onto the path and back up the shale to my cave. I'm trapped, alone, and on a strange planet, that I'll never get off.

The second stage of Rome's fast-forwarding programme was altogether different from the first. Data of experiences, knowledge, and language would download directly into her mind as both it and her body grew, but I had needed to create sensory data too, she couldn't learn, function, or even live without these. I wrote a rain forest with croaking frogs and leaping monkeys, flashing videos of myself talking, explaining all sorts of things and recordings and photographs of the little I had of Cind. I wrote about elephants trumpeting to the sun, children playing having fun, bats and owls flying underneath the moon, cacti silently swaying on yellow sand dunes, puppets dancing to the strum of guitars, light and glitter glowing from twinkling stars, rainbows, waterfalls, mountains and skies and teddy bears and unicorns whispering soft lullabies. Everything and anything that was pleasant and pleasing she would have, and she'd be safe and entertained as she grew. I began the programme and my whole living room turned into idyllic countryside with green meadows dotted with dandelions and buttercups with the noise of singing birds and buzzing bees.

"It's now or never." I said and voiced the fast-forwarding to begin. All the colours immediately mingled into one and all that I could see was a blur of blue and black, with Rome in the middle moving her head about rapidly, jarring it from the right to the left and to the right again. She would reach the age of seven in just under a day. I knew I had done all I could and exhausted I collapsed into bed.

My clock read 8.28 am. I had been asleep for a good 20 hours. Rome would be around the age of six. Eager, I went to my living room. Through the blur of blue and black, there she was laying, naked and still on the floor clutching herself, shivering, with her back turned towards me. Something was wrong. I voiced the programme to stop and everything vanished but her.

"Little one," I whispered, "Rome?"

She stayed still on the bare floor. I picked up a cotton gowny and gently placed it over her. As I did, she turned her head round to face me. She looked just like Cind when she was a child with the same freckled cheeks and curly, blonde hair, but her eyes. They were strained and bloodshot. "Rome...Rome...it's me… your Daddy."

She didn't answer, she just stared at me, but I waited, and then after what seemed like an eternity, she spoke.

"Are...you...real?" She asked.

"Yes, real as anything little one and I'm here to look after you."

Her forehead wrinkled as she mulled this over.

"How can I trust you're real?" She said.

"You just have to believe me. I'd never lie to you."

She turned back round and clutched onto her gowny as a cold

sadness drew over me. I had known from the beginning that her virtual world would be imperfect, I just didn't have the time to programme even simple things like clothing or food. To do that, with Rome fast-forwarding and also growing, it would have been so complex it would have taken years to write. But weren't these very basic things what a child needs for stimulation and growth and sheer pleasure? Wasn't it their birth right, even an artificial one? But it had worked. It had! She was conscious and could communicate and had character, I knew this even by knowing her for only a few seconds.

"Have they gone now?" She asked.

"Who?"

"The monsters."

"The monsters?"

"Yes, the ones that look like creatures but don't move the same. They're always here. Have they gone now?"

"Yes, they've gone now, and they're never coming back." I said, not knowing what she meant.

"Really?" She said turning back now a little animated. "I always thought they'd be here." She said getting onto her feet. "They're liars and mimics. They mimic everything. The animals...the children..." And then she slowed down and looked at me nervously

"And...even...you... You're not a monster now, are you?"

"No. No. I swear darling, I swear. Look," I said kneeling down so that I was eye-level with her and extended my arm, "Feel my hand, I'm all flesh and blood."

Hesitantly, she touched my hand then she smiled and retracted her hand sharply.

"Are you *really* real?"

"Yes."

"My *real* Daddy?"

"Yes little one, and I always will be."

She mused this over and a huge smile spread on her face.

"And Mummy, my real Mummy, will I see her too?"

"Yes, you'll see her soon."

"How soon?"

"Soon darling, real soon." I said and put the gowny on her properly and tied the belt at her waist.

"Tell me. These mimic monsters. Tell me what they're like? How are they different from the real animals?" I said changing the subject.

She looked about my living room, absorbed by the sofa and the light and the window.

"They take the place of real animals, the elephants and the dolphins and the foxes and the bees. But they don't move the same. They move really, really, slowly and they don't sound the same too. That's how I think you must be real. You move properly and you can talk properly too. Are you sure they aren't coming back?"

"Yes, never." I promised. Numbers began rolling around my head. I checked the programming. Damn! Through exhaustion or stress, I had made a tiny error. I had been a few digits out from Rome's consciousness and the things that I had written in Rome's world, but that tiny error, multiplied by 210, was gigantic. The animals and the children and even the blowing leaves and water flowing in the streams would have been all out of sync and would have appeared really, really, slow to her. Not real. Lies. Mimics.

She walked precociously to the window and stared down onto the street hypnotized by the people and vehicles rushing by.

"Where is this?" she asked.

"This is the big wide world honey." I said and picked her up into my arms. Whatever she had gone through, whatever I had put her through, she was going to be alright and I knew then that I would do anything for her to find just a little bit of peace. I could feel warmth, I could feel life. It *had* worked, it had.

I'm feeling down. Real down. I don't know if I'll ever make it to another dome, and even if I did, I may find nothing there. I stare and stare at the words, and the paintings and think and think. What does it all mean? I've got to figure it out. I've gotta try to remember, and maybe, somehow, I'll find my daughter and my suit.

I'm suddenly aware of a presence. It's Buttercup. He has an uncanny way of appearing without warning. He has two fresh pods with him and after I greet him, he twists an orange one open and makes a gesture for me to drink from it and then passes it to me. I gulp at it, thankfully. God it's good. Creamy, banana sort of thing. Like a milkshake, and it's cold too.

"What are we going to do my friend?" I ask him. He cocks his head, not understanding my words and chirps at me and stares back and then his irises dot about his black eyes like he's thinking hard.

"What would happen my friend, if I did indeed leave the fog?" His big eyes stare back at me, blankly. I take another swig, "And how *can* I leave anyway?" He breathes in and his vibrant green vocal sack enlarges and then shrinks slowly making a disheartened and exasperated sound like he just doesn't really know. He picks up the other pod, a clean white thing and twists the top off and then takes a handful of the flesh out and offers it to me and chirps as he does. He's saying, "Eat. Eat. It's good." And I take half of it from his hand and both of us chew on it. It's good. Like warm, salty, peanut butter, and we swallow, and then at the same time both laugh.

"HUU, HUU. HU" He laughs deeply. He's really a kind creature, caring for me like he does. And through him, I'm better understanding them. After we've eaten, he beckons to me with his hand. He wants me to go down to the dome with him.

"I suppose I can't stay here for the rest of my days and let this cave become my tomb…can I!" I say and with a little bit more hope, walk down with him.

Over the next week I get in the routine of feeding the whites. My tolerance to the pollen gets stronger and stronger and I can stay for hours now, without being affected, but I don't know if breathing in so much is doing me any good. My skin is taking on a yellowish colour, maybe the start of cirrhosis or something!

I wander about one day and get closer and closer to their dome's centre. And with each closer step, I realise they aren't pushing me away. I walk to it, and this time, I'm not stopped. Underneath the roof that they peel back, where they sing to the stars, I see there's an abundance of vines and leaves and orchids growing there. Something glints in the sun, right at the top. It's my visor. My suit is up there! I excitedly voice it on, but it doesn't power up so I try again, but still no use. It's probably been damaged somehow I think so I start climbing, overjoyed, up the vines to retrieve it, but something in the dense foliage catches my eye. What is that? There's slight movement and a sound. A heavy breathing sound. And I see them. Eyes. Huge black eyes opening. I'm taken aback and nearly fall. Something alive is hiding there and I quicken my pace, but those huge black eyes are flushed with red, and I'm back in my cave. What was that thing? I really don't know, but whatever it is doesn't matter, I've found it. I've found my suit.

    We stayed by that window for hours then and I marvelled at her being mesmerised by the mundane everyday passing by on the street below. She was so inquisitive and ravenous for knowledge and asked question after question, about the Sun and the wind and the sky, about the people and children and dogs walking by, about dragons and princesses and shining knights, and how things worked, like gravity and kites, but most of all, she asked about Cind. Why wasn't she here? What was her favourite colour? Where was she? How old is she? What was she doing and when would she see her? I managed to evade the truth quite well, I mean, what was I going to say? "Your Mum's on the other side of the galaxy just now and by every passing second she's speeding further and further away from you and is never coming back, never going to see you and doesn't even know that you exist?"
    Evading her questions, we flipped through images of clothes for her to wear whilst for the first time, she sucked on a cold, virtual, frothy, chocolate shake. She loved it, and she made her fashion choices through slurps and burps. She picked black woollen boots, white tights and a red dress with her favourite animal embroidered onto it. An eagle flying in the night sky. With a voice, it all

materialised and clothed her. She was so excited about it, she jumped up and down on the couch and did twirls on the rug. She tried popcorn and pasta and toffee pudding with dollops of whipped cream and later, with both of us in complete silence, I combed her beautiful blonde curls whilst looking deep into her bright, blue eyes. After a while, she stopped me brushing her hair and she got up with a little frown on her face.

"What is it Rome?"

She let out a little moan and said "My ideas. They should have come by now." Her eyes darted about the room, panicked. "They *are* coming, aren't they?"

"It's OK, calm down. What do you mean? What are your ideas?"

"My ideas. They come in my head every day. Why haven't they come?" She cried. She seemed frightened, lost, and then I got it. The data, the damn data that downloaded directly into her brain, she called them her "ideas."

"You know, you don't need them now. You can learn and live without them you can..." But she burst into tears and cried out "No, no! Don't tell me I can't have them. I need them, please Daddy, please."

"OK, OK, just give me a second." I said and voiced the programme on to look through the other downloads that hadn't been used. She hopped around the room impatiently as I worked. Changing the speed of them, and double checking them so I knew I would get it right, I voiced it on. As the data transferred into her mind, Rome's panic instantly dissolved. She relaxed into the rug, cross-legged and seemed to be in complete bliss, but I found it a little disturbing. It was like a junky getting their fix. Sadly, it was probably the only thing in her world that she had used to look forward to. After a couple of minutes, she fell into a deep sleep on the rug. I picked her up, put her onto the sofa and gently pulled a blanket over her. Most people, maybe everyone, is addicted to something. Whether its booze, work, jogging or beans, my little one was addicted to knowledge.

I had to help her so the next day I decided to run a school simulation with a teacher and children sat at desks. As they materialised, Rome watched intrigued, but she seemed bewildered by it all. The teacher asked Rome if she'd like to sit down, but Rome ignored her. She then ran over to me and said, "Where did they come from?"

I thought carefully about my words. "They're virtual Rome. The teacher and the children aren't real, but they act out just like any real person would. Do you not want to give it a go? It could be fun and much better than one of your ideas."

She stood, solemn, thinking, and then her lip trembled and tears filled her eyes.

"Am I like them?"

God, what was I going to say? "No, no darling I swear… you're nothing like them."

"You're lying, I know you are," She sobbed, "I just appeared like them and I know I'm not a real child. A real child has a real Mummy and a real Daddy and they don't see monsters and they don't have ideas. I'm not real, am I?"

"Yes, yes, you are real Rome. Real as anything. Look." I said extending my hand. "Feel."

"I don't want to."

"Please Rome. Please."

After a few seconds she extended her trembling hand and gently held mine.

"You can feel it, yes? You can feel my hand. What do you feel?"

She thought for a few seconds, unsure and then said, "I can feel your fingers, and they're soft and warm."

"See. VR simulations can't do that. They can say that they're feeling a soft and warm hand, but they can't actually feel it. But you can, can't you?"

"Yes." She said happier thinking this over. We kept touching hands with her fingers clasping mine.

"And you can see me with your big, beautiful eyes. You can hear

37

me with your little, cute ears. You can sniff through your tiny, little nose and breathe the air in all around you." I said. She was calm now, entranced by it all, but then she retracted her hand sharply.

"But I'm not real! Am I?"

"I'll be honest Rome. You're not like other children but you *are* real." I said sitting down next to her. "You know there was a man, a very wise man from a long time ago that said 'I think, therefore I am,' you think don't you Rome, so because you do, that makes you real. Real as anybody, you just don't have real flesh and real blood. It's just virtual. Wonderous. Magical."

She let out a chuckle and then frowned.

"I saw it. I saw what you said. But then it left."

I let out a laugh too. "That's what happened to me when I first heard it and it never came back. See, you're just like me," I said. "And we don't need any silly school simulations if you don't want one. We can go on the web if you like?"

"The web?"

"Yes. It's an information portal. You can find out about anything. I know you'll love it." I said voicing it on, "What would you like to know about? Anything, anything at all."

"I want to find out where Mummy is."

God, I just wasn't going to get around this and maybe it was better to get it over with, sooner, rather than later.

"Well, before we do, I think I need to explain some things about your Mummy and how you *are* different." I said picking her up onto my lap.

"You see I copied you when you were small and still in Mummy's tummy." I said patting her tummy. "Then I tried to make a world for you to grow in. You see, you are real but you're different. You're virtual. A virtual being." I said with her quiet, taking it in. "And Mummy didn't know I had done it, and although we'll contact her very soon, she doesn't know that you're alive, but when the time is right, we'll let her know and she'll be so, so happy."

"So Mummy doesn't even know I'm here?"

"No, not yet, but she will very soon. "

"And if you copied me," she said "what happened to the real me?"

God. How was I going to explain this?

"Well." I said carefully choosing my words. "You weren't going to make it in this world...so I... copied you... so that you could." I said. She mulled this over. I didn't know if she understood.

"Mummy didn't want me, did she?" God! I thought hard about how to reply but Rome was adding it all up and she said horrified "What happened to the real me?"

"Look little one, you weren't going to be, you just couldn't, so I saved you."

"This world," she said, "It's false, just like the teachers and the children. This world isn't real, is it?"

"No, of course it is, in the VR…" I stumbled looking for the right words.

"In the VR?" She said with every little piece of the jigsaw fitting into place. "Switch it off. Switch it off. I want to see what I am really like."

I had no other choice. I had to let her see. I voiced it off and we were back in my bare living room and as I did, her clothes vanished, and she was naked again. She tried to clutch herself, but her hands went straight through herself. She was stunned and stared at her hands and her bare body. I came over to her and moved my hands through her intangible ones.

"See, you're magical." I said moving my fingers through hers. They shimmered as they moved in and out.

"You said I am real, as I can feel. But without the VR I can't. You lied Daddy, you lied. I'm not real. I'm not real at all." She shouted and ran out of the room and hid in the bathroom.

I breathe in the clean air of my cave, excited. My suit. I've finally found it and it's close by. But what was that creature hiding in the foliage? And why haven't it and they given my suit back? They must know I need it. I've gotta stay calm and focused, and I've gotta find out what that thing is.

I cautiously go back down to the dome and amble, slowly, towards the centre. I'm not stopped so I sit cross-legged away a bit from it and watch. I see him. He's a huge thing, hidden by all the foliage and he's like the yellows and the whites but bigger, maybe 25 feet tall and fat. Real fat. He's black all over except for his throat which is a deep purple. And his eyes. They're huge too. Over a metre in diameter and I'm sure he's staring right at me.

There's an enormous pile of pods there and a yellow comes and picks one up and unpeeled throws it up into the air. The black one's mouth snaps shut around it, swallows it whole and then deeply chirps for another. I make out he's wearing a crown of vines and orchids like the whites. He's like a fat, huge, lazy king.

I try and discreetly voice my suit on. It doesn't power up though and after I try again, louder, it still doesn't work. Something's wrong with it, or maybe it's just out of juice. The king stares again, watching my every move. I've gotta be prudent, so I go over to the yellow and make gestures that I want to take over the feeding, and he lets me, and so does the king.

I have to use both hands to throw the pods up to him. They're damn heavy and the pile is huge. I wonder how many he can eat in one day and I point at my suit and make hand signals that it's mine and I need it, but he just chirps for more fruit. I need to get it. And after a decent hour of feeding him, he falls asleep in the safety and shelter of his den of vines and flowers.

I stay there that night, right next to him, and come up with a plan. Whilst they're all asleep, I'll try and get it back and then take it to the cave where I can get a good look at it and find out why it's not powering up. Clambering up the vines, quietly and carefully I ascend, through the chirping and tweeting snores, slowly, I get right close to it, nearly in touching range when he awakens. He sees me and deeply growls and grabs a hold of me. And then he squeezes and squeezes me, drawing the very air out of my lungs and his eyes turn that red again and I'm back in the cave. I collapse onto the ground and just lie there. This is impossible.

    The next few days were real tough. Rome had become so withdrawn she didn't want to do anything. She didn't try any food or drink, she didn't want to go on the web and she didn't even cry for her ideas. She spent a lot of the time hidden in the bathroom but when she was in my company and I tried to make conversation with her, she mostly ignored me. I added to her programming so that the clothes she had picked would always now be on her. As they appeared, she raised her head from her slumber and acknowledged them with a grunt, at least she would always be dressed.
    I nervously read the news about other VB's. The police were searching and rounding them up. People didn't know what to do with them. One side was for freedom and the other was for execution. People were scared, that was for sure and some VB's had reportedly gone into the main frame. Their minds uploaded into the clouds. Their consciousness's hidden in the wires. But what was I going to do about Rome? I had to get her out of her depression and I toyed with the idea of taking her outside. It was a huge risk but perhaps one worth taking. Yes, I must. I went and told her my idea and she raised her head and said "Really?" So, we got ready, and nervously I opened the front door. For the very first time, Rome ventured outside of our studio. We walked down the steps of the building and already she was intrigued with just that, standing amazed just by the stone steps of the staircase. We came to the exit and went outside and the rush and hum of it all hit her. Cars and motorcycles grumbled by, men and women and children passed and went into the chippys and bars and bakeries. Birds flew above and rested in the trees. Rome was entranced by it all, amazed, staring at everything. We passed a toy and sweet shop and she peered into the window looking at the dolls and teddy bears and lollipops and chews. She fed into the wireless energy masts, so theoretically, she could go anywhere on Earth. But we could never be found out! We ambled on into the

town's park and saw ducks and squirrels and dogwalkers and cyclists.

I was more at ease now and was thrilled at her enjoyment. But then some kids came running around us with water pistols spraying each other. Rome smiled at them but one of them squirted her. The water went straight through her making her shimmer.

"Hey Matty," He shouted, "Check this out." and he sprayed her more and his friends came over and did the same. Rome just stood there, frightened, shimmering.

"I think it's time to go." I said. Then a little one started prodding her with a stick.

"She's not real." One of them said and Rome started to get upset. People started staring. We were creating a scene and Rome started to cry but she still stayed stood there.

"Just a basic hologram" I said nervously. The expressions on people's faces were unsettling. "Right, time to go Rome." I said, "Right. Now." I said sternly and we both paced off. "Hurry. Hurry." I said. We darted down an alley, passed the back of a steamy, restaurant kitchen and by wobbling, rubbish bins and quickly got back to our studio. Rome was really upset.

"I'm just a basic hologram you said. That's all I am? And all the people are scared of me." She wept and ran and hid in the bathroom again.

We couldn't go out again, that was for sure, but Rome was distressed and depressed by it all. I didn't know what to do to help her. Pacing around my living room I came up with an idea. To ease her pain, I stayed up and wrote a programme that could turn web data into data that could directly download into her consciousness. It would hopefully be like one of her ideas, and theoretically, it could work for any site. After another sleepless night, I tried to get her interested.

"Try it. You can find out about whatever you want, even your Mummy" I said. That caught her interest, so we sat on the couch and I started it up. All the data I had of Cind and all her digital footprint too would download directly into her mind. I voiced it to begin, and within a couple of seconds, Rome's eyes widened, her body shivered and then she relaxed. Tears filled her eyes.

"I can see her, I can see her in my mind, and I know about her. She's out there, somewhere in space right now and she doesn't even know I'm here." She said and hugged me, "And she didn't want me. I knew that before, but I see now... I see...how big a mistake she thinks she's made and how much pain she's in." She wept. "And you've *always* wanted me."

"We'll get through it Rome. Together."
"Always?"
"Always."

I go back down and I'm allowed to feed the king again. He's calmed down but stares at me with a look of disgust as I throw up to him, pod after pod. Eventually, after about fifty of them, he signals to me through shakes of the head and chirps that he's had his fill. I'm so close to my suit. It's just stuck up there, in arms reach, hidden in his crown of flowers. I point to it and then point to myself and say, "*My* suit…*Mine*." But his beady black eyes just stare back vacantly.

"By hook or by crook, I'm gonna get it." I say to him. "My daughter. Rome. Do you understand? I need my suit. To see my Rome!" And after a few seconds his purple voice sack inflates, and he purrs out, "Rommme."

I jump up, "Yes, Rome. You *do* understand."

He then reaches for my suit and plucks it from his crown. Then he shakes it at me, pointing to it and then to me.

"Rommme." He purrs.

"Yes. Rome. My daughter. To see her I need that." I say pointing to it. He looks like he's thinking something over and after a while, he places my suit, ever so gently onto the ground. And then he starts tweeting and chirping and pointing to it and to the sky. I cautiously go over to him. I've gotta slow down. I can't mess this up. I voice it on, but it still doesn't work but I get my hands on it and pick it up. Finally, I've got a hold of it. I start checking it out, but the king suddenly gets irate and pushes me back and picks my suit back up. And he growls at me, enraged for who knows what and he puts it back in his crown. What have I done wrong? What does he want? And he keeps growling and staring. A yellow appears and pulls me away. It's Buttercup but I try and fend him off. I'm so close, but he's stronger and he's right. I've gotta stay calm. I've gotta be patient. I plod back to my cave, thoughts swirling around my head. I *will* get my suit.

I go back to feeding the whites and over the next days watch the yellows pass their sacks to the whites which are then carefully placed into their pouches. They're creating and growing life but what does the king do? He's just a gigantic, lazy, oaf that gets mollycoddled by all the yellows. And he has my suit, *and* my daughter. I loathe him.

Rome began getting into my programme in a big way, but after the web pages data downloaded into her mind, she immediately wanted another. I tried to get her to slow down a bit, but she wouldn't.

"Another." she'd say and then after two seconds "Another." and "Another." She was so persistent and I just gave in. I let her take full control, and in trepidation, watching, curled on the corner of the couch, she learnt, books of all kinds, politics, sciences, theories and philosophies, you name it, all in the blink of an eye. I didn't know what she would become, with her child's mind with such complexities and dark truths about humanity. But she couldn't get enough and she didn't sleep and got her fix, one after the other, again and again, never tiring, never talking and then after six days she finally stopped.

"I've learnt it." She said.
"What?"
"Everything."

"Everything? What do you mean?"

"I mean I've learnt everything, worth knowing or not."

I didn't know what to say. She didn't seem like a child anymore.

"Are you happy then?" I asked her, "Have you found peace?" She stood up and walked towards the mirror.

"I don't know if happiness or peace was ever intended for me" She said and then she began getting taller and taller, changing in front of my very eyes until she was a couple of inches taller than me. Her body curved at the hips and she grew a bosom. Her skin changed too, to a metallic silver colour, streaked with light blues. And her hair turned to burning fire. Her strands flickered about like red and yellow and green dancing flames Then her hair changed back to her original blonde curls, but they floated and slowly swirled around her head as though she was submerged underwater.

"I think I prefer this, don't you?"

"What do you want Rome? What can I do for you?"

"I must leave. I need to see the world and I can't do that confined here."

I'd been thinking about this all the time she had been downloading. I knew she had to see the real world no matter how large the risk.

"We can go to the farm. We'll come up with an excuse or something." I said "We'll say you have a disease...a disease like leprosy or something where you're fragile, breakable and can never be touched. You'll see your Grandparents." I said. I knew we would get caught, it would only be a matter of time, but we'd try our hardest to make it last as long as possible.

"I'd like that." She said.

"But you can't go like that." I kind of half laughed.

And with that her skin changed back to a normal colour, her hair fell back hanging to her shoulders and a white dress covered in pastille flowers appeared and clothed her and black boots donned her feet.

"This?" She said. She looked so much like Cind.

"Yes. That's perfect." I said, and that was that. We lightly packed said our good riddance to the studio and left. We got a taxi and safely, with no problems, got to the farm. I took Mum and Dad to one side and explained how my "friend" Rome had a disease where she couldn't be touched. I think they were suspicious and they went to talk in private.

"This is where you grew up then?" Rome asked.

"Yes, my home. Your home."

She walked around interested in the furnishings and pictures and ceramics. My parents came back and gave us the go ahead.

"You can stay as long as you want." They said. I felt guilty about all the lies we told them, but there had been no other way.

They put on a fresh spread. Tomatoes on the vine, cheeses, chutneys, freshly baked bread, olives, grapes and much more, but I said Rome was on a special diet and couldn't eat our food. They were taken aback a little but after a bit of social awkwardness, everything eased and the talk around the dinner table flowed. And Rome evaded or came up with plausible answers to Mum and Dad's constant questions. I would just have to remember her lies!

After we had eaten, I took Rome for a stroll through the meadows and the forest. And we went to the glade with the twisted trees.

"It's paradise." She said, "And I feel such a strong connection to all of this, like somehow, I've been here before."

"This is where I first met your mother." I said and I told her of the super toys and the fairies.

"I know," she said, "Somehow I know."

I took her to Cind's old house, and we talked and talked and lay in the tall grasses and watched the sun dip and the moon and stars appear and glow bright. Rome pointed to and gave the names to all the constellations that I didn't know, and I shared my dream of going to space with her. I went on and on about it, how I had always wanted to go, and about my time at the space academy and how my dream would never come true now but how her mother had succeeded and was out there right now, millions and millions of

46

miles away. I pointed in the direction Cind would roughly be.
"I feel happy." She said, and so did I.

Whilst feeding the last of the fruit to one of the whites, Buttercup comes up to me and starts chirping at me, dead excited like. He grabs a hold of my hand and pulls me near the centre where there's no rocks or foliage. A lot of the yellows are congregating there, maybe 40 or so and they all surround me in a circle. I'm kind of nervous and musing what it's all about when all their eyes get flushed with that blood red, and from under the dome, we are suddenly somewhere completely different.

I'm blasted with cold and I see snow gently falling, carpeting the ground and coating all the trees. I'm in an enormous forest and the air is clean and pure and not tainted by any pollen. I look up to the sky. It's changed. There's a different sun up there. They can hop, naturally, to other planets! And I have no idea where in the universe I am.

The yellows, all start buzzing about, chitchatting, and getting busy. They climb the snow laden trees, to the pods that are abundantly growing from thick branches. I realise now. They harvest their food from different planets. And through different cycles, I bet they can get it all year round. And I'm sure I was right. They all join forces together for bigger hops. Maybe to everywhere and anywhere.

I see Buttercup, jumping up and down in excitement so much he's weeing onto the white snow. He pushes me and chirps and tweets and points towards a tree, laden with pods, I know what he wants and I start clambering up it. It's cold, but I feel vitalised. I am somewhere completely different and new, and I am apart of them.

All of them, start chirping and whistling as they work. It reminds me of the seven dwarfs just loving being busy. They pluck the ripe and different coloured pods off the trees and fling them all onto a pile on the ground. They're so fast and I only manage to get one to all their fives, but at least I'm helping.

After only an hour, we gather an enormous pile and then all the yellows rest and sit in the snow and crack open some of the pods. There's blue ones, grey ones and white ones, but they only open the blue ones. There's liquid inside and they take huge swigs and pass them to each other down a line. When one is passed to me, I take a big slurp and splutter and laugh. It tastes fruity but has a real kick to it, and after a few minutes it hits me and I'm tipsy. And all of them are singing and rolling about in the snow laughing and I cry and giggle and scream and shout, and for the first time in a while, I feel happy.

After the fun, Buttercup guides me to the pile of pods and they all surround me and it and their eyes are flushed with that red and we are back under the dome. The heat warms me, and the yellows start doling out the fruit to the whites and the king, and I stay by him and start feeding him. I can see it. Up in his crown. It's so close it's almost winking at me.

Days went by, dancing and singing, walking and fishing and me digging the dirt with Rome by my side. We chatted so much then about everything and anything. About what came first the flowers or the bees, about the magic of a chrysalis and a caterpillar key about what could ever be on the other side of a black hole and what the heck anyway was the purpose to it all? I think she finally found a little peace then, and that time was so, so special to both of us, but as I had known, that all changed on a Friday afternoon when I was painting the barn roof. Rome suddenly ran out of the house shouting.

"WE HAVE TO LEAVE."

"Why, why? What's happened? "

"Now Arow, we have to go now."

I went to talk with Mum and Dad, but they were too upset and all they said in answer to my persistent questions was how could I have no respect for their lives and their beliefs and left me to go and pack and leave. Of course, I knew they had found out about Rome, but it had been worth it. But now, back in the studio, everything became bleak and awkward. It felt like it had become a prison and days slowly trickled by like treacle running down a rotten apple. We didn't use the VR and Rome didn't speak, she mostly meditated and slept. I tried again and again to talk with her and find out exactly what had happened on the farm, but to no avail. A fortnight passed which felt more like two months when she finally opened up.

"We were in the kitchen whilst you were working, just me and your father and we were talking about space travel and could luddites not approve of technology when it comes to this. To venture into space, to learn new knowledge and to find life and perhaps even another intelligent race. Your father said no, and he couldn't understand why humanity couldn't be happy with its lot here on Earth. To live off the land and be patient that the bigger questions would all be answered one day, anyway. And we got onto the riddle of souls and he said the how and why, that he believed in reincarnation and if somebody died in space or on another planet, how could their soul, millions and millions of miles away, find their way back to Earth? I was considering that I didn't even have a soul when the neighbour's dog came running in and jumped up at me and went straight through. Your father looked horrified as the dog kept jumping through me, playing. Aghast he asked, "What are you?" but his expression, I'll never forget that. Like I was abhorrent. A fiend. The Devil herself. It cut deep into me Arow, and that's when I ran to you. I realised then that I was never meant to be and now I don't want to." She said. "I want you to do something for me Arow, something you must."

"What...anything...anything at all."

"I want you to turn me off and delete all my data."

My head flopped down, "I can't do that Rome...not that."

"Please Arow...please."

"I'm sorry, I just can't. I can't murder my own daughter."

She went to the window and looked up towards the sky.

"Then you can do something else for me."

"Yes… whatever you want… anything but that."

"I want you to let me go. I want to go into the wires to be with my own kind. And you have to delete all my data so I can't come back."

"There must be something else." I sobbed, but I knew she wouldn't change her mind and I had no other choice. I had to let her go.

"OK, I will." I eventually said.

"The programme is already set. All you have to do is say my name and delete, and I'll be gone."

"But will I ever see you again?"

"Yes. But I don't know when."

I voiced the VR on and went over to her and embraced her. Both our fingers entwined.

"I'll miss you little one, promise me you'll come back."

"I will."

I looked deep into her eyes and then said. "Computer. Rome. Delete." And she began to fade, "Look out for our gifts." Her last words were before her body blew away into wisps of colour like dandelions blown away by a gentle breeze until I was clutching onto nothing apart from glitter which turned to embers and then to nothing at all. All was lost now, all was gone.

As the months passed by, I went mad in my studio pacing the floorboards and pulling at my hair. Searching the web one day, I found that on one of the planet's a sweet fruit had been found which was a calming sedative. I synthed one and tried it and it seemed to help. I fell into my sofa and into my bed and it got me through the days as I searched for any sign of Rome or the other VB's. I decided to tell Cind everything. I sent her a message, not knowing when it would reach her, and then went to Mum and Dad's, with my tail between my legs and sobbing, I told them everything.

I was safe on the farm, but I had to keep a check on the VB's and any sign of Rome so I went back and forth from the farm and my studio. More months passed without any sign, until one day, something special happened. Links to data were sent all around the world where amazing technologies had been invented, like pills that extended a person's life spam tenfold, theories proving the existence of other dimensions, equations not put to the test yet but for the possibility of time travel and most importantly to me, suits, that enabled a person or more, with its own batteries to last years, to hop through space. I knew it was the VB's, possibly Rome? And now I could eventually live my dream and go into the black, but without Rome? I just couldn't. But one of the tech-gadgets gave me some relief. It could scan someone's mind and turn their memories into 3D holographic films so I recorded all the good times with Rome, when she was young and a lot on the farm and ate my fruit and watched me and her when we were happy and I sank deeper and deeper into my couch.

    I hop daily with the yellows to different planets harvesting different fruits. And I get better at it. Three pods now to every five of theirs. And we venture to such different and diverse worlds, on alien soils. Snow, sand, and rock. Around rivers, seas, and lakes. On top of crags, hills, and cliffs and under pink rainclouds, green suns, and blue moons. I immerse myself in my work and these strange places. I didn't expect I would be doing it like this but I'm doing what I have always dreamed of.

    On a warm planet, out in a jungle, we get on with the gathering. There's black fruit and green ones that we pile up, but after half an hour or so, I see a different, smaller one, way up at the top of a tree. It's golden, and for some reason, I really want it. I climb up into the branches and reach out for the fruit, but I realise, seeing through all the thick foliage, it's right over a precipice. I'm unafraid though, and although something is niggling at me that I'm doing a real stupid thing, I climb higher and higher, but as I do, the tree starts to bend.

    It's dangerous but I'm so close and I'm sure if I just go a little higher, I'll get my hands on it. I climb a little bit more, but the branch starts to drape and before I decide to go back down, the branch bends right over the precipice and I'm hanging there. There's a creaking sound, and I shout out to the yellows, but after a crack, I'm holding onto the branch, in mid-air. In the blink of an eye, I know I'm a gonna. But I can't die yet! I've gotta see Rome, even if it's just for one last time. But it's about 100 feet down and when I come to the sudden realisation that my end maybe could be for the better, I splash into, crashing, foaming, water. I go under and try and swim up and when I resurface, I cough and splutter. There's a strong current and I'm getting whisked away down the river. I yell to Buttercup and the others but go down under again. I keep getting dragged under but I fight it. I'm not…going…to…die. I just manage to keep above and eventually the wild river calms, and I land, sapped of all energy, on a black, sandy shore.

    I lie there, coughing out water. I'm alright, I think, but I must have been in the river for a good 20 minutes and Buttercup and the others are probably miles away and have no idea what has happened to me or where I am. Would they really care though? I'm not sure. Surely they would, but either way, I am completely, and utterly, lost.

    There's no sign of Rome anywhere but a bit of good news comes. Funny. She's yet to read the message I had sent her, but she'd already sent me one. Cind! Her and her crew had found a planet and settled on it and Cind contacted me before it had hit the headlines. Being a botanist, she'd hit the jackpot. There was no animal life there but an abundance of plant life. Strange silvery shrubs that shook by themselves on the windless red meadows, fast moving mosses and lichens that crawled into the waters during the day to cool down and feed on tiny dust particles and then crawl back onto the rocks to sleep at night. But what really got her going were these trees. Gigantic things, over 700 feet tall with trunks as wide as a mansion. She'd dated them, and the biggest ones were over 14 thousand years old! And at their trunk's bottoms, stacked up on the red grasses, giant fruits were growing. Inside, they found they were brimming full of this juice high in an acid like the citric acid found in a lemon, but much stronger. The top branches were of a metallic type and were growing downwards towards the fruit, and Cind and her team were waiting, surmising the branches were coming down to feed into the fruit like a lemon battery, to power something, but what? They're just waiting for it, real excited like and she says she misses me and I'm happy for her, I really am.

I was humming and hawing about leaving. I desperately wanted to go, but what about Rome? She said I'd see her again, so I had to wait for her, I just *had* to. I chose the colour and the size of my suit anyway. The arms, legs and helmet, a bright yellow, and the rest, a jet-black. And then I synthed all the parts and slowly put them together. I marvelled at its completion. The metal alloy was hard, but light and the suit was compact, sleek, maybe even indestructible. I tried it on. It was snug, but real, real comfortable.

As the days ticked by, I enviously read about the other hoppers that were already on their way. Anybody, no matter how old or with what ability that wanted to go could simply synth a suit and hop off. And it was spreading like wildfire. People grabbed at their own lines of exploration and it became unfashionable to go on a same line. If you picked someone else's line but changed it by just a fraction of a degree, by the time you hopped a few times, hundreds of thousands of miles, you would be hundreds of miles away from that person and the distance would only increase as you ventured on. And the possibilities of all of us finding new planets and new life only magnified, by billions.

And then a message arrived. An amazing, life altering message. It simply said, "Go Arow, go and live your dream and go into the black and I'll join it too. Have faith." It was Rome, without a doubt. She was out there, somewhere, and somehow, she knew of my dilemma and would somehow join me. So that was that. I went and said my last farewells to my folks, went back to my studio and had one last look about and put my suit on and voiced it to hop.

And there I was. Finally, in my still black. Below, green and blue with swirls of white and grey she twirled and danced, just for me. Marvellous. Fascinating. Absolutely inconceivable. I stayed there, above her, appreciating her and meditated in a silence I'd never known the like. Calming, peaceful, tranquil, she revolved around and around whilst all that I could hear was my own heavy breathing, in and out, and in and out, and in and out. I stayed there for hours, hypnotised by her, taking it all in. And then I practiced using the suit, moving around using its blasters, zooming in and out with its telescopes and inflating its bubble.

My bubble was my lifeline. An 18-foot sphere that with a command, inflated from and deflated back into my suit. I would live inside it for my journey. I could safely take my suit off in it and breathe, and sleep, and synth any food and drink and eat, contact anybody, and check on the net and even watch telly. It also had a VR function but that was the last thing that I wanted to risk. To gamble with my sanity. The bubble would always scan through space, so it would read any incoming asteroids or debris and automatically hop away from harm.

I practiced how to move about inside it. Floating about when the false gravity wasn't on, and when it was, I practiced walking about. It was intelligent and somehow it automatically knew what I wanted to do through my thoughts and actions. Its inner shell would change to what I desired. Flattening when I wanted to stand or jog and forming a seat when I wanted to relax. When I needed to sleep, it formed a bed and with a word I easily synthed a pillow and a duvet, and then I'd simply de-synth the pillow and duvet back into the battery supply. Energy. That was the key. It was going go be a long, long, journey and I had to think about that. The suit and the bubble's outer shell acted as a solar panel to replenish my battery, but the amount I would use for synthing oxygen, water, food, hopping (especially the hopping) and all the rest could never be fully replenished. I was on a timer. A negative one. But the battery alone would probably last 20 years, so I did have time. And if I was out there stuck, I could always stop hopping, conserve my supplies and re-charge. But in the end, it would never last. And the further I hopped away from Earth, the more and more likely it would be that I would never see her again. I was on a one-way journey, but I was damn excited about it.

The sun's beginning to dip and I'm wet, cold, and utterly lost. I pick myself up off the black, sandy shore and brush myself down. Buttercup and the others are nowhere in sight, and I'm scared. I could be anywhere, anywhere on this planet and anywhere in the universe. I fall down, weak and tired and cry out. I just want to see my daughter.

I decide to climb a tree, but I'm so drained, I climb slowly. And I slip back and forth on the slippery bark and nearly fall, but eventually, get high up. All I can see up there is thick jungle. It's no use. Where are they?

I shout out, to Buttercup and the others but my lonely voice just echoes back at me. I'm going to have to camp up for the night so I go back down and start picking up branches to make a den. But I'm not alone. I see movement in the trees and hear noises. They've found me, I think, elated. But no. There's strange panting sounds and no tweeting. Then I see it. Red and yellow striped fur, and big, like a puma. He opens his mouth, yawning, pulling pink gums back to show off large, sharp, incisors. It's a four-footed creature, and his teeth aren't those of a vegetarian. I try and scramble up the tree again, but there's another one, already up there, growling back at me so I slip back down.

I pick up a stick and start shouting at the one on the ground whilst keeping an eye on the one in the tree. Then, as I see a third as the one up the tree leaps down near me, snarling. They circle me, ready to pounce, so I strike the one closest on its nose. It yelps but doesn't back off. I look about. There are stones on the ground so with my spare hand, I pick one up and throw it at them. But they're unafraid, growling, and getting ready. I throw more stones and get one right in the eye, but it just snarls, enraged so I throw more. One stone hit's a large rock and sparks fly off it and hits one of them. It gets startled, scared! So I quickly bend down and pick up two of the stones and strike them together. Sparks fly off and the creatures stop their advancing. I hammer the stones together, quicker, and with more force and sparks fly off igniting the foliage. Yes, I have fire, and the leaves and bracken are so dry, I've quickly got a blaze. Smoke pours upward and I shout at the creatures, waving my stick next to my fire and the creatures yelp and run off.

I've beaten them, but I lay down beaten myself. The heat feels good but quickly it gets uncomfortably hot. I get up again on staggery feet as the flames spread fast and surround me. Real fast as the leaves and bracken are so dry. Smoke now is everywhere, and I violently cough. I've gotta get away from it, but I can't see because of the smoke. I'm trapped and I can't see a way out. It's everywhere. I shout out again, "BUTTERECUP!" but it's no use. I could try and jump through it but I'm sure I'd be a gonna. I'm a gonna anyway. I get ready to jump, but as I run up, the heat is too much, scorching my face. I retreat, my eyes dart about, searching for a way out through the thick smoke and flames. It really is hopeless I think and scream as my skin begins to sizzle. This really is it.

I wanted to get close to Cind as possible but without being rude, so I copied her line and became probably the first person to stalk someone in space. I deflated my bubble, voiced the co-ordinates and was off. I was on my way, and after only a few hops, I leapfrogged passed Jupiter. I zig-zagged as close to the other planets as possible too and paused to see Saturn's magnificent rings. The rock and ice caught by the planet's force was mesmerising. God my heart was pounding. And then I hopped further on, passed Pluto's orbit, and after only a day, I was out of our solar system and into almost virgin black. My excitement became deflated on my 14th day though. Relaxing, watching an old black n white in my bubble, eating spicy chicken wings and corn on the cob, I received a message. It was from Cind. She'd finally got, *and* replied to my message, but she sounded pissed, real pissed. It was all about Rome.

"How could I?" she said, "How she felt violated," and "how I'd ruined her life," and "had gone against the laws of nature." I was hurt, real hurt, but I knew I had had it coming and to be honest, I mostly felt good about it. I was on my way now and she knew everything. I had no secrets, I no longer needed to lie. And she would get over it… I hoped. So I sent her the 3D films of Rome. It would take a while, but she'd see… she'd understand…wouldn't she?

I was in contact with some of the other hoppers. One guy who I got on with wasn't too far away, relatively speaking, with only a delay of 12 hours. He was called Eddy and he was completely honest with me and I was with him. Pressure got to him mind and he'd gone a little loop da loop. His violent drunken love of his life, who had always attacked him came at him one night. But this time quiet Eddy retaliated, for the very first time, after many trips to A & E, by cracking him over the head with a potted plant. He killed him. And not wanting to do time and thinking Earth had nothing left for him, he synthed a suit and hopped off. He was going to look about for a bit on "walkabout" as he called it, before directly hopping into the heart of a star. Poor sod.

I looked out for other hopper's messages and films too, to see where they all were and what they'd found. Fascinating the reasons why and how they left their home world. Many a night I watched the films I had of Rome and one night, missing her, wondering when and how she would eventually find me, I fell into a deep slumber. Dreaming, I was awoken by a hologram.

"Arow. Arow. It's me." I heard her gently whisper, but as I came to, confused by the film and her, I realised there were two of them. It really was her!

"ROME!" I shouted out and voiced the bubble's VR on. "How? How can it be?" I said, embracing her "God I've missed you. How on Earth are you here?"

"Arow! Daddy! I'm so happy."

"God so am I." I cried, overjoyed, "But how are you here?"

"I wrote a homing programme into your synth box. And when I left the ship, I streamed myself to your suit."

"Ship? What ship? How? You've been gone so long." I said and she told me. When she left me and went into the wires, she found her own kind. Hidden, they watched humanity, through cameras and screens and they communicated with each other and created humanity some gifts. It wasn't hard, she said, just joining up old technologies and theories and just adding to them together and advancing them. They came up with the suits. They thought it was every man's right to explore space and find worlds and just live freely. They wanted to help. And they wanted it for themselves too. After a short time, she sent herself to Cind's ship. She needed to see her, and months went by with Rome having no consciousness, she was just heedless zeroes and ones speeding through space towards her mother. But when she got to Cind's ship, and awoke in the ship's data bank, she hadn't felt anything at all, from being switched off and turned on again, she realised she mustn't have a soul. How could she? Just on and off, black and white, but I tried to explain she couldn't prove that, but she wouldn't have it. The proof was in the pudding. Now in Cind's ship, Rome finally saw her mother in flesh and blood. She watched, unnoticed through the ship's cams but she was too afraid to show herself, and then everything changed. Rome was there, looking through her computer cam at her mother when she received and read my message.

"My own mother never wanted me! I can't get over it." Rome sobbed.

"It's OK little one," I said cuddling her, "You've got me."

Flames are burning, scorching my body and face and I'm lost in the thick smoke. Above the noise of the crackling and spitting burning bracken I hear an animal of some sort, moaning and howling. It's familiar, and I hear chirping and tweeting. Sounds fast and panicked.

"HELP! HELP!" I shout out as my hair catches alight and my skin sears. I start screaming. It's so painful and my eyes are blinded. And then suddenly I feel no heat, just sheer agony. I can't see but feel hands on me and hear their startled and alarmed chirps. And then silence and I'm suddenly blasted by cold. I'm on the ground, writhing about and just see white everywhere. It's snow and hands rub the cold all over my face and body. It's soothing.

I come to, lying on the ground with yellows all around me. My face and body is caked in snow and now I'm cold. It's so much better though and I see I'm under the dome and Buttercup's pet comes over, wagging its tail and moans and howls familiarly. *You found me* I realise, and I let him lick me whilst Buttercup looks proud as punch, but at the same time, deeply saddened.

"Thankyou." I manage to croak through burnt, sore lips. And he whimpers and cries. At his side is an orchid and he picks it up. It's brimming with pollen and although I try to resist it, he makes me drink from it. It actually doesn't taste that bad. I'm so used to it now and a warmth goes through my entire body. And then I feel faint and close my eyes.

Don't know how long I've been out but the pain is a lot less. I look at my hands, they're a raw red but although being scarred, they'll heal. And thank God I can see. Not sure if I'm hallucinating or not. I don't think I am. I hear voices but it's them. I do have a strong tolerance to the pollen now.

Over the next days, I get pampered and Buttercup makes it his main duty to feed *me*. Mainly a lot of pollen and cold, sweet, sorbets and quickly, the soreness and blisters lessen and lessen and my body miraculously recovers. Something of good may be in the pollen after all and soon I'm back on my feet. I amble over to the king and look up at my suit whilst he stares back at me.

"Somehow, I *am* going to get that." I say, and he chirps, belly laughing whilst a yellow throws pods up to him.

And so, we were coupled on a one-way mission deep into the still black. Me and my whole being connected to my suit and so too was Rome. She now could only exist from the power from the battery in my suit, but we were together and venturing where practically no one ever had. After that night, we both hopped off, together, and hopeful. In the coming days we got further and further away from the only thing we had ever known and the Sun became smaller and smaller and more like a star seen from Earth, and after only 20 months, we left the Milky Way and were into Andromeda. I felt like I had lost some part of me. Home had vanished.

But I got another message from Cind, and she didn't sound upset in this one, she sounded alive. The branches of her enormous trees *had* pierced into their giant fruits, and they were right, it was to power something. At the very tops of the trees, high in the sky, flowers bloomed, but these weren't just any old flowers, they had lenses. And that night, the flowers projected dancing lights into the sky. She said the lights danced and communicated through sounds to each other, and there didn't seem to be any other reason for why they did this, apart from their need to talk with each other. Talking trees! And it was over in a matter of hours and wouldn't happen again for the planet's year. She was astounded and said it reminded her of when we first met, with her super-toy and her fairies, but these were the real thing. It got her thinking too, about Rome. And Cind asked questions about her. She was interested now, but Rome was not.

"It's a beginning." I said, but Rome was silent. Just too damn hurt.

Over the next years, we saw so much, maybe too much, and maybe too fast. Water vapour clouds dancing in space, and the sunlight making rainbows in the black, the thousands of comets we passed, with frozen ice and bacteria on their backs, the birth of new planets and the death of the old and dried up riverbeds with secrets never to be told. But I eventually used most of the suit's juice. To be safe, so I knew I had enough power to synth necessities, oxygen and water and food, I would wait 7 hours in the still black, charging up from the different suns, and then hop. And hopping and synthing used a lot of juice.

We saw it then. How the whole Milky Way is forever slowly spiralling towards its own black hole and then in time, other galaxies would swirl into that too. Joining, growing, and spreading into one supermassive black hole. Like cream, in black coffee, swirled by a spoon, billions of trillions of years away in time. And those black holes would suck in more planets and suns and more black holes until eventually they would widen into one immense gargantuan hole sucking in the whole universe and compressing and changing everything into something completely different and to be spat out somewhere entirely new. And we were sharing every hopper's data, collating it. We'd fucking begun mapping out the universe itself! Yes, only a grain of sand in a vast sea, but still a start. Then, after years of going deeper and deeper into the black, we found her, our pearl. My suit scouted out a planet which had water, vegetation, a breathable atmosphere, and a good chance of life. Complex animal life. We hopped above her and looked down with our telescopes, we were mesmerised by the large land mass, rivers, seas, and tropical foliage.

"Life is down there." Rome said, and we spotted the domes. "Intelligent."

We just stared down, stunned.

"This is going to change *everything*."

I make a full recovery from my burns and blisters and I sleep under the dome every night. I feel like I've become one of them and I understand them more and more. I differentiate between the chirps and tweets and clicks and get to know words and phrases. And with Buttercup, although it's difficult, I practice mimicking their words, tweeting them back to them.

I get back on with the harvesting and feeding the whites, and now and again, the king. One day I see all the yellows all surround the king and a swollen white with a creature inside of her. They hop and are gone for hours and when they eventually come back, I see the creature is gone from the white's empty, flabby, belly and the King looks battered. His whole belly is torn, flesh is hanging off and he hides in his den of flowers seeming like he's been in a cage fight with a wild animal. And there he sleeps.

At night, the moon and the stars are so much bigger and brighter. And every night I listen to them all singing to the heavens, and them telling their stories. And I start understanding most of it. They sing about their ancestors and how the yellows create life and the whites nurture it. It's like a lottery to them, they never know what life they will create but all the worlds that they visit, they explore and remember to send that exact life to. It's like a puzzle to them. A whole way of life. To create new life and find the perfect environment to fit, and they've been doing it for eons.

The pollen's consuming me and I feel like I'm somehow changing. I still am me and hopefully always will be, but my mind has changed, but strangely, it seems it's for the better. I'm not so bogged down with my old way of thinking and for probably the first time in my life I experience real, pure joy. And even though I still so want to get my suit and Rome back, my anguish and anxiety is becoming less and less. What will be, will be.

And I sing with them. I sing about this new life and my old life on Earth. I sing about the green hills and misty mountains and blue skies. I sing about fresh bread, and strong lager, and live rock'n'roll. I sing about humanities conquests, their building of bridges across rivers and travels and adventures to the stars. But most of all, I sing about Cind, Rome and my folks. And down here, underneath my dome, I will stay.

Looking down, using the telescope, we saw the jungle far below was like a living, swaying, rainbow. There were giant flowers down there. On the ground and in the trees and up in the canopy. I scanned the air, it was breathable, but a poison tainted it. A powerful hallucinogen that probably was being made by the flowers. Rome agreed, so I'd have to keep my suit on at all times.

"Well, do you want to go down and meet them?" Rome asked.

"I don't know. Now I'm here I'm kind of scared. I'm damn excited, but what happens if they don't want to be found? What happens if they're aggressive? What happens if we taint *them*?"

"They can't hurt me. And your suite will protect you. And if it gets rough, we'll hop off. And we need to make contact. We must. This is the beginning. Come on. This is history in the making."

"But what do you think? They're intelligent, but they must be kind of primitive if they just live under wooden domes. It'll probably get sticky."

"Just because they live under wooden domes doesn't make them primitive. Looks can be deceiving. Think of Gran and Grandad. And anyway, even if they are primitive, it doesn't make them hostile."

I looked down, building myself up with butterflies flapping around my belly. "OK, what's the plan?"

"We'll hop half a mile from that dome." She said pointing her finger. "We'll check the place out and those flowers, and then slowly walk towards the dome, as peaceful as we can. Weighing it up, I'm pretty sure they're not primitive."

"OK, let's do it." I said and voiced my suit, and from up in the silent stillness, for the first time in years, I was suddenly flung onto hard, solid ground. I felt kind of giddy, and nauseous, but I knew it wouldn't last. We looked about. The jungle was thick with strange foliage and a thin purple-grey mist was in and all around the air. We heard this slow, haunting, flapping.

"Look." Rome said and she pointed to these giant butterflies, with probably a 7-foot wingspan slowly flapping through the air. They were amazing, beautiful, and dazzling in different colours, shades and patterns. I was mesmerised as I watched one avoid the tree's giant thorns and delicately land in a safe place and suck at the pollen from one of the flowers. They didn't even seem to have noticed us, but that was good. Then I noticed these little bird-like creatures, loads of them, about the size of swallows but with two sets of wings. They buzzed whilst they hovered in the air. More insectoid like. They had 3 pairs of stick legs and they nestled on the trees and sucked at something sticky dribbling down the bark. On the ground, I was careful. Something was writhing underneath all the leaves and bracken. Saw eyes and feet sticking out now and again. Everything was so alive and noisy and busy. The whole jungle was alive with colour, movement and sounds. The low flap-flap of the butterflies, the buzz of the swallows and the crunching of the creatures moving underfoot. And then I made out other noises. Chirps and clicks and tweets. They sounded different from the rest. And there was the noise of branches creaking and moaning under a weight.

"They're coming." Rome said, "They know we're here."

"Who? The inhabitants?" I said. I felt like I was being watched. Flashes of eyes staring. I could hear them communicating with their chirps, and then I saw one. God I was overcome with sheer terror and excitement. Fucking aliens!

They were humanoid, about 4 feet in height and all naked. They were a bright yellow colour, except at their throats, which was a lime green and they had rippling muscles and huge black eyes, the size of grapefruits with bright coloured irises. They were in the trees, swinging from the branches and making it look easy, avoiding the giant thorns. More came, about 20 of them and they jumped down onto the ground. They surrounded us, all noisy like. Their green throats inflating and then deflating like a toad. They stared at us, inquisitive and unafraid as they chirped and tweeted at each other. Then some of their eyes changed from black to red, and then vanished right in front of our eyes and others appeared out of thin air. Fascinating. Without the aid of any technology, they could hop!

I'm initiated under the dome and become one of them. Everyone's there, Buttercup and the other yellows and whites and the king. And they are all ecstatic. Even the king who's healed from his battles seems less gloomy. And I'm donned in a crown of vines and orchids and they all sing and we drink the pollen from the flowers and the booze from the pods and eat and drink and chirp and tweet. I love the pollen now and thrive on it.

And with my new mind, I can only see the positive in life and I can't believe how I ever saw the negative. That's got nothing to do with nothing now and has no useful purpose at all. How could I have ever seen it that other way? Watching them dance and revelling and singing, I marvel at their way of life and see how important their work is. How can creating and growing life and taking it to a perfect world and creating new ecosystems be nothing less than the most important purpose that exists? And when did it all begin?

I ask Buttercup about the king. Where did he go? What role does he play? And what happened to him? But he evades my questions and I think he says something like "Time will tell." And he teaches me about their ways. How they get completely drained after big hops and how their diet rejuvenates them. That's why they have such a strong craving for sugar. And that's what they do. Eat and gulp on sugary pods, sweeter than toffee or honey. And the worlds and places they go. They're all stored in their mind since they first began exploring. Each planet, he explains, has a particular and distinct scent to it. Or maybe more like flavour, it's hard for me to understand. They have indescribable maps of the stars in their minds, and I will go with them.

The inhabitants ushered Rome and me through the dense jungle until we got to their dome. Underneath, we see other ones, white ones that were completely different from the yellows. Bigger, over 9 feet tall with really thick tree trunk shaped legs. All pure white except at their throats which was a bright pink. I noticed a lot of them had these big bulging bellies, and something was inside, something alive! They were all cleaning themselves with their long black tongues, until they saw us. Then they all stopped, pricked their heads up and stared at us inquisitively with charcoal eyes the size of melons. The yellows seemed to be the males and the whites the females, but Rome whispered they may have a complete different sexual system to us.

They offered us food and drink, these giant fruits and seemed sad when Rome didn't take any, but when I scanned it and knew it was safe, I did. And when I hopped it inside my suit to eat and drink, it was delicious. They found this fascinating, and they found Rome fascinating too. They couldn't get enough of moving their hands through her body. They seemed to laugh as they did this. Deep reverberating belly laughs, through their vocal sacks. They were captivated with me too. They kind of looked in awe touching my suit and my helmet.

After a while, they ushered us to the centre of their dome. There was a load of foliage growing there including many of the bright coloured orchids, but something was beneath. I made out feet and then arms, and then a huge belly and massive black eyes. It was another one, over 20 feet tall hidden under all the foliage. It was jet black, with a purple throat and a huge hand suddenly burst out, and before I knew it, it grabbed a hold of me.

"Don't hop." Rome said, but it was kind of hard not to. Whatever it was, it had a strong grasp and I didn't know what it wanted with me. Lunch? It brought me right up close to it's face. It was like the others, but huge, and it stared at me and gave me a shake and then licked me with its huge, wet, tongue.

"ARE YOU SURE ROME?"

"Yes, just wait." But I was scared. Shit scared and the cacophony of excited chirps and tweets made it more so. The yellows and whites were practically rolling about on the floor. Then the black one let out this deep boom of a laugh and then placed me back onto the ground.

"I think he likes you." Rome said but he kept his eyes on me. Really unnerving like and then all of them started that belly laughing again.

That first day, Rome started to get to know them.

"Their clicks and chirps and tweets sound simple, like a bird's song." She said, "But it's a sophisticated complex language."

She began to copy and sing back to them, learning all the time. That night, I projected films into the centre of the dome of our home. Of blooming flowers and fruiting green trees, and of bubbling brooks and crashing white seas, and of our red brick houses and of our giant, glimmering skyscrapers and of our astronauts and clowns and brave, lion tamers, and of goldfish and hamsters and dogs and cats and of strange alien beings dressed in clothes and hats, and they all watched, spellbound, pointing, absorbed and then chatted and laughed whilst Rome tried to explain things, mainly in one-word phrases she'd somehow, already picked up. What really tickled them was Earth's diverse animal life. They couldn't get enough and watch amazed and asked question after question to Rome who tried to explain with her limited knowledge.

"They keep asking about Earth's continents and how and more importantly to them, why animal life is unique to each one."

As the night drew in, they unfolded the centre of the dome with poles and lacings right where the huge black one was, and all of them, sang up to the stars. The black one seemed to be obsessed with me. His gaze followed me wherever I went.

"They're singing about their ancestors, and about far-off flung worlds that have fallen long ago." Rome said. She seemed alive once again and I stayed up late and happy, and hopeful, I slept soundly. Rome didn't, she continued learning their language and walked about all night chirping and tweeting and studying and testing. When I woke, Rome explained that there seemed to be only one black one underneath that dome. She thought there'd be one to each dome dotted on the planet, like a hierarchy, and I watched bemused as the yellow's picked up fruit pods from a giant pile and one by one flung them to the black one who caught them in his mouth. He's like a king. A lazy, fat, greedy one, getting waited on hand and foot, and he always had at least one, beady eye on me.

Rome studied all of them and ran tests. "They're farmers" she said. "Not in the typical sense though. They're farmers of life." The yellows, she thought, were creators. They have sacks, where a person's genitalia are and they grow until they're ripen and fall off. Then they are carefully and quickly taken to a white and are placed into their liquid filled pouches. They're like marsupials. Nurturers. But it's not just their own kind that develop in these pouches. It's any kind of life. Mammal, reptile, fish, bird or completely alien and although Rome didn't yet know what role the king played, she presumed it was vital.

After a few days, Rome could pretty much talk their language. She was intrigued by the king and she'd sit by his side and have long discussions with him. One time, she broke down upset.

"What is it?" I ask.

"I need to chew something over. Just need to be by myself for a bit." She said and disappeared into the jungle.

"What are you up to?" I said to the king. And what was he? Rome was gone for hours, but when she finally did come back, she said, "I know what part the king plays. He's vital in their society. And he could do something incredible for me."

"What can they do? Tell me."

"They can give me something, something I've always dreamed of and something I thought I could never have…they can give me a soul."

"What? How can they do that? Are you sure? I don't trust him Rome."

"No, he's not lying. And he can."

"Well do it. Let them try."

"No… we can't."

"Why?"

"Because there's a deal. They want something in return."

"What. We'll give them whatever they want."

"No. It's something that is impossible. Something we'd have to sacrifice. Something *you'd* have to sacrifice."

"What? Whatever it is I will give." Rome looked up to the orange-blood sun.

"I knew you'd say that." She said. "But they want your suit. They've never seen the like of it and are awestruck by it. And that's their deal. For me to get a soul, they want your suit."

"What do they want with it?"

"I'm not sure. A word keeps coming up I'm not sure of 'mother' I think? They want to tweak it and do something with it I'm not yet quite sure of."

"We can synth all the parts of another suit, we can give them that."

"It will take too much energy. All the parts and another battery that has no power. Months of charging. Maybe over a year. And they don't want to wait. The deal is they want it now."

"Then if they want *my* suit, I'll be stuck here, yes?"

"Yes"

"And will I survive?"

"Yes. But you'll be consumed by the pollen and I just can't let you do that."

I think it over. I've travelled so far and I'm tired now. All my love and dreams are in Rome. I needed to do it.

"I'm over 40 now Rome and I'm already so damn tired. I need to give you this. You're my daughter, my own flesh and blood. Whatever they want me to do, I'll do it."

Rome was silent for a minute.

"No. I can't let that happen. The pollen will drive you mad and you'd be trapped on this planet…forever."

"You know I'd do anything for you. Let me."

"No. We can't. You can't."

I was near the king and he still had his beady eye on me. That's why his gaze always followed. He didn't want me, he wanted my suit. I walked over to him.

"Here. Have it. Just fulfil your promise." I said and unscrewed my helmet and started to take my suit off. The pollen immediately went deep into my lungs and I coughed and spluttered and immediately felt high.

"No Arow. Please… you can't."

"I must!" I said as the king shimmied about excitedly. He was eventually going to get what he had always wanted.

"NO!" Rome screamed. "Put it back on." I collapsed onto the ground and everything started swaying and shaking.

"OK, I give in, we'll give them your suit. But not like this. You need to get prepared. Please, put it back on."

"I give in." I said and screwed my helmet back on, but the king got irate and chirped loud and angrily at me like he'd been hoodwinked by something. He picked me up by my feet and jostled me about. I felt sick as I inhaled the sweet oxygen from my suit and I threw up in my visor. I just made out Rome shouting something back to the king and eventually, and thankfully he stopped shaking me and put me back onto the ground.

"I need to do this Rome." And she was silent, thinking.

"At first you'll be overcome by the pollen." She said, "You'll be sick, and you'll hallucinate and have memory loss. But over time you'll get accustomed to it. But you'll change Arow."

I voiced a command and the vomit from my visor vanished and I could see her again.

"Change? How?"

"I think, if you are sure you want to do this, it's better you find out for yourself. Are you sure about this Arow?"

"Yes. I must"

She was silent and then said, "We'll do the preparations today. We leave tomorrow."

"Where are we going?"

"To my planet."

Buttercup's teaching me well and I'm really getting a hang of their language. I love chatting to the energetic, excitable yellows about their harvesting of fruit all over the universe and the mellow, slow, whites who relish being waited on hand and foot and care so much about the creatures that they nurture and shape inside themselves. We talk about everything and nothing and more, and I even start getting on with and start chatting to the king. He's old. Real old and has seen so many different moons and suns. And through him, Buttercup, the whites and the other yellows, my memories start slowly trickling back. About what happened to my suit and where Rome went. I can see her. On her new planet, with the others and how we got her there and how she has become what she has become. But I need to remember more. Why isn't my suit powering up?

I stare and stare at the paintings and the cave graffiti on the wall, "IF I LEFT THE FOG," What am I missing? Remember Arow, remember. And slowly memories *do* come back. I remember after I came back from Rome's planet and when I gave up my suit. I programmed the password to be *typed* in! I rush down the hill and down to the dome and to the King.

"I have to type it in." I chirp to him, "I programmed the suit's password only to be *typed* in." The king's eyes widen and his huge hand comes out from behind his flowers and vines and he plucks the suit from his crown and sets it before me. I open the suit's arm revealing the keyboard and carefully type "IF I LEFT THE FOG," whilst the king rocks back and forward with excitement. Me and him have been waiting for such a long time for this, but as I hit the enter key, and wait, it still doesn't power up. I type it in again. It's gotta work, it's just gotta, but still, nothing. I look up at the king and chirp to him. He's deeply saddened and so am I. It doesn't work, and probably never will.

Rome scouted out a cave, extremely close to our dome but high upon a rocky hill. She said once we were back, I must wait there.

"If you stay above the pollen, it won't be such a shock to your system." She said. "It'll take days, maybe even weeks, so you'll need supplies."

We went to my cave. It was pretty damn depressing seeing it, but I didn't let on to Rome about my feelings. I synthed food in containers and water in drinking vessels and also paint and brushes. I wanted to cave paint, not just for entertainment, but if I did have memory loss, I wanted to remember. And then we went back down to the dome where they were all waiting for us. The yellows and the whites and the king. The king nudged a short yellow one towards me. He had beautiful black eyes with yellow and orange and gold irises and had an animal of some sort, sitting on his shoulder.

"This young one is going to be a sort of guardian to you. They don't want you around whilst you're confused by the pollen and he'll keep you on the right path. He's been gone a while, learning their tricks."

"Hello." I said, and he beamed a big toothless grin at me. He had such magnificent eyes. Me and Rome were then ushered to the centre of the dome, and the yellows and whites surrounded me and Rome and the king in a ring.

"They all join their powers for really big hops. And this is a real big one. You ready?" Rome asked, and before I could answer, all of their eyes were filled with that blood red and I was suddenly blasted by rain and gale. It was dark, and thunder grumbled, but lighting strook again and again, lighting everything up every couple of seconds. I'd never seen a storm as fierce.

"THIS IS YOUR PLANET?" I shouted above the noise.

"YES... ISN'T IT WONDERFUL."

All the yellows and whites started going mad, dancing, and splashing in the rain and singing to the heavens. Then they all surrounded the seated king who beckoned Rome towards him.

"THIS IS IT THEN." She shouted and walked over to him, she then turned her head and shouted, "BE PATIENT." And she walked straight through him and inside of him. He closed his eyes, then began swaying from left to right. I went to him, and above the roar of the storm, I heard gurgles and bubbles popping inside his belly. I didn't know what the Hell was happening, but I had to have faith. I had to. The yellows and whites sat down in the wet and joined him swaying back and forth, and I sat down and joined them too.

Hours went by, and thankfully, the storm began to calm. I could see the planet clearer now. There were these giant silver poles, hundreds of feet high, dotted about the landscape and as the lighting flashed, they lit up, absorbing the energy. Organic, lightning conductors! Below, whatever was on the ground, flashed and glowed in waves. This place was so fierce and peculiar, but also so beautiful. All the ground was a carpet of pulsating colour. Pure energy. And it gave me an idea. If I could somehow tap into it, I could charge my suit and synth another one. All might not be lost.

I got dozens of messages there whilst waiting, I must have been closer on this planet to many of the other hoppers and I got one from Cind. It had been sent 4 years ago and as a sleepy red sun rose its head over the silver sandy mountains, I read. She babbled on about Rome. How wrong she had been and how she must see her. She wanted our co-ordinates and wanted to synth a suit and meet us. Suddenly something howled. It was the king. He collapsed onto the wet ground and writhed about in agony. Then his belly burst open and what looked like his innards fell onto the ground. The others came to his aid whilst horrified, I watched on as whatever had come out of him started to move about in the goo. I saw a figure.

"CIND? CIND? IS THAT YOU?" I shouted. I rushed over, and a slimy hand came out to greet me which I grabbed onto. It was solid! And then a head came up and I wiped away the goo from it. A face. A solid face.

"It's worked." She said and I helped her to get on her feet. She stood and tried to shake off the goo.

"How can this be?"

"It's like VR. But realer". She said, spitting out the muck from her mouth. But I'm completely bewildered as more hands come out and. Rome helped another figure get onto their feet and I helped with another. Cind is solid, and there were other beings?

"This is what the King does." Cind said, "He's a tweaker… *and* a copier. Every creature that the white's nurture, the king can tweak inside him to suit a planets condition. IT'S THEIR GREATEST GAME." She shouted excitedly, "To grow life, any, and all kinds, and to find a perfect planet with the perfect habitat for them. They've known about this planet for millennia and never thought they could find life for her…until they met us."

There were three other beings all cleaning the purple goo from themselves. All humanoid, all solid, all like Cind. Two males, and another female.

"They can't speak yet, I have to teach them, but they're my own kind." She said. "Everything's a conductor here. We can go into the trees and grasses and bushes. Into the seas and rivers and waterfalls. Into the clouds and storms and droplets of rain. Even into the ground, and the rocks and deep down into the lava. And we can come and go as we please. We can be touchable, *and* untouchable. We can sense. We can eat. We can feel the wet and the cold and create fire to warm ourselves and cook our food. And we can taste our food, and get nutrients from it. And we can touch each other, and reproduce, and not just our own life. We can be farmers of life ourselves. I'll be a part of this planet now, always and I will die here, but not my energy, not my children, not my soul."

"I'm so happy for you. You've finally got what you wanted." I said and embraced her, "But I got a message. It's Cind. She wants our coordinates; she wants to come for you."

"Give her your planets. Let her come and find you, and maybe one day she'll find me."

"I was thinking. If I could somehow tap into the power…"

"No. It's too risky. You could blow the whole suit, and you promised them."

"But…"

"Trust me, you're going on an adventure yourself."

"What of the King though? Will he live?"

"Yes, that's what he does. He'll need time and pampering to recuperate, but he'll be fine. He's been doing this for decades."

The others, Rome's companions, cleaned themselves in the water puddles and splashed and grinned at each other. I went to them and shook their hands and they smiled back at me. They seemed childlike.

"This is it then." Rome said, "*You* have to go back, and *we* have to go."

"But will I ever see you again?"

"Time will tell. Goodbye Daddy." She said, and as she did, before my eyes, her companions glowed bright, then sparkled and vanished into their world.

"Goodbye little one." And she smiled and sparkled and vanished too, leaving only fading embers that were whisked away by the breeze. I took one last look at her planet, *their* planet, and I knew all would be well. Then the yellows and whites surrounded the King and me, and their eyes changed to that colour and we were back under the dome.

The king crawled back under his flowers and leaves. He had flapping skin where they had burst from, but his vital parts seemed all intact. I had to give my suit up then, but before I did, I voiced a last message to Cind, telling her everything and with the coordinates of my planet. Who knew when she'd receive it.

The king chirped weakly at me and slowly unfolded a hand.

"Yes. You'll get it." I said whilst he watched. Half-heartedly I took off my helmet and immediately the pollen hit my lungs and my mind. I started taking my suit off, but I forgot, as everything began to sway and swirl in colour, I needed to assign the suit to the king. But no…why should I? Cind is coming and I must see her. But I can't. We made a deal. Rome's deal. I bent over and vomited. All the whites and yellows weren't what they seemed. They were demons. How could I have been that stupid? They've tricked me and tricked Rome. And the king. What foul creature was he? No, don't let it consume you. You have to hold on, you have to give the suit to him. I voiced in a password, but I made it so that it had to be typed in. Then I giggled, "Have your cake and eat it." I said and flung it at him.

He picked it up, looked at it, tweeted at it, and then shook it about like a baby with a doll. Then he stared at me and let out a sad howl. All of them chirped and tweeted, screaming at me as I stumbled away, away from them and away from their dome. I staggered onwards being sick as I went and somehow got the bottom of the hill. In a daze, I started to climb. I had to get away before it was too late.

I eventually got to the top and breathed in the air thankfully. Have to keep a hold, have to remember, but things were slipping away. Like sand, falling in an hourglass, I was hanging onto every grain of my mind. Fighting my confusion, I picked up a brush and started painting on the cave wall. The password. The damn password I've got to write, but the letters were all muddled up. I don't want to remember, but I have to. I will not write it. I'll paint the letters but not the phrase. Yes, I know what to do and I paint "IF I LEFT THE FOG". That's fitting, isn't it? And will I ever? They will never know nor never have Rome or me. I paint my suit, bright yellow on black. That damn king and his brothers and sisters may have me, but never truly. And with my last energy, I painted Rome and her family and her electric world and then collapsed onto the cold, wet floor.

I remember. I do. Taking Rome to her planet and her getting tweaked and copied. And I remember her and her kin vanishing into their very own personalised world. Their electronic world and how the inhabitants, my new family, found it for her. They are all happy and she is finally at peace, but my password doesn't work. Why? There's still something yet for my mind to reveal.

I stare and stare at the words and the letters on the cave wall. Remember Arow. Remember. Phrases and smells and sounds and words and places and faces begin to resurface. Faces from my past. Childhood friends on the farm. My folks and their neighbours and their friends and their dogs and horses and cats and Patsy the milking cow. Pals and tutors in the space academy. Eddy and the other hoppers, that idiot from Cind's take off and of course Cind and Rome. Then I remember passed Earth. The loneliness of space and feeling so fragile but at the same time experiencing overwhelming silence and peace. And then the thrill of Rome joining me and travelling and then finding our planet. And meeting the yellows, and the whites and the king and why and how I gave up my lifeline. Why I gave up my suite and how I couldn't ever give up Rome. Yes, it finally clicks. "IF I LEFT THE FOG." It's an anagram. In a confused and drugged state and not wanting to finally let go of Rome, I programmed the damn thing and painted the letters as an anagram. I run down the shale bank giddy and quickly get onto my path and sprint through the jungle and down to the dome, right to the king.

"IT'S AN ANAGRAM." I shout to him, "A FUCKING ANAGRAM! I couldn't let her go, I had to hold on to her. I just couldn't lose her for good, I couldn't give her up, but I haven't, and never will. I see that now and I can go to her now whenever I want. And I can hop all over the universe. Maybe even back home." I say as the king takes my suit out from his crown of flowers and places it down at my feet. I flip open the arm, and on the keys, with a long finger, I type in "THE GIFT OF LIFE". After all this time, I hear the grumble of my suit powering up and the king chirps out and belly laughs and swallows the suit whole. That was their deal. He couldn't copy my suit, but he could tweak it. To enable it not to just synth food or water or air... but life.

I think of Rome, and codes dancing in shimmering light and reproducing and learning and philosophising about all the big questions, about what this everything is really all about. And I feel calm. The king finally splurges out the new and improved suit and we watch it power up for the last time and then vanish from this planet and into the silent black. An empty suit, travelling for all eternity now, recharging from the energy of different sun after sun after sun. To create new life, in and around the everywhere.

Printed in Great Britain
by Amazon